Pictures Or It
Didn't Happen

Pictures Or It Didn't Happen

Sophie Hannah

HODDER

First published in Great Britain in 2015 by Hodder & Stoughton
An Hachette UK company

1

A CIP catalogue record for this title is
available from the British Library

Paperback ISBN 978 1 473 60353 0
eBook ISBN 978 1 473 60354 7

Typeset in ITC Stone Serif Std by Palimpsest Book
Production Limited, Falkirk, Stirlingshire

Printed and bound by Clays Ltd, St Ives plc

Hodder & Stoughton policy is to use papers that are natural,
renewable and recyclable products and made from wood grown
in sustainable forests. The logging and manufacturing processes
are expected to conform to the environmental regulations
of the country of origin.

Hodder & Stoughton Ltd
338 Euston Road
London NW1 3BH

www.hodder.co.uk

For Chris Gribble, who knows
why – at least as much as I do.

1

'I don't believe this, Mum!' Freya wails at me. 'Please say you're joking!'

I am not joking. She must be able to see that from my face.

No, no, no.

It can't be true. I can't have screwed up so badly.

Except I have. I've forgotten the music for Freya's audition. *No, no, no, no, no . . .*

I didn't exactly forget it. Not completely. I remembered to put it in the car. Then I was so stupid that I can't actually believe it. I left it there. *I left it in the bloody car.* Now, when I urgently need it to be safely inside my bag, it's in the Grand Arcade car park.

I'm an idiot. Worse than an idiot. I am every bad thing.

A harsh, skin-chilling wind whips around my head. My hair hits my face like lashes from a cold whip. Cambridge is always either much warmer than everywhere else or much colder. Today, it's like a Russian winter.

'What are we going to do?' Freya demands. Her eyes are wide with panic. I know what she's hoping for: any answer that isn't 'There's nothing we can do. It's too late.'

She's been practising her song for weeks – recording herself, then listening to each recording, making notes on how to improve her vocal performance.

Freya is nine. She's known since the age of five that she wants to be a singer. This will be the first time she puts her voice to the test. I'm terrified of how crushed she'll be if she fails. 'I *cannot* mess this up, Mum,' she's been saying every five minutes since she woke up this morning. 'I *have* to get in. They *have* to say yes.'

Now, thanks to me, she's going to miss her chance to try. I've failed on her behalf. She can't audition without her music, which her brainless mother has left in the bloody, fucking car. It was the only thing that mattered, the one crucial thing I had to do . . .

My teeth are chattering from the cold. At the same time, my neck is too hot beneath my poncho. I wonder if I'm about to faint.

'Mum!' Freya's voice pulls me back. 'What are we going to *do*?'

Think, Chloe. Quickly. You have to solve this problem, and the seconds are ticking by . . .

It's like a Maths problem from one of Freya's homework sheets. I look at my watch. We're about ten minutes away from where the auditions are happening. It would take us ten minutes to walk back to the car park – ten minutes in the opposite direction. Freya's audition is in twelve minutes.

'We'll have to run back to the car and get the music!' she says, blinking hard, trying not to cry. 'Come on! Don't just stand there!'

'There's no time, Freya. Unless we suddenly both learn to fly, we won't make it. We'll miss your slot.' My heart thumps in my mouth. I tell myself that this isn't a life-or-death crisis. But it feels like one.

I look at my watch again, desperately hoping time will have started to race backwards. It hasn't.

'We can't go back, okay?' I say, struggling to stay calm.

'We *have* to!'

'We *can't*! We only have twelve minutes! It's not long enough. You read the letter: anyone who misses their allotted time – tough luck, they're out.'

People are staring at us as we stand on Bridge Street shouting at each other. 'Freya, listen. I know this feels like a disaster, but—'

3

'It *is* a disaster! How can I sing without my music?'

'You'll have to manage. Look, we'll pick another song – one that whoever's playing the piano will definitely know. It's not ideal, but—'

'Like what?' Freya demands. 'What song?'

'I don't know! "Happy Birthday To You", or—'

'No way.' My daughter's face hardens. I feel like the worst kind of traitor. 'Do you even *know* how embarrassing that would be, Mum? "Happy *Birthday*"? No! I can't *believe* you left the music in the car! *Why* did I trust you? Give me your keys!' She holds out her hand. 'Without you slowing me down, I can run back to the car and still get to the audition by half past.'

'No way! You absolutely could not. And anyway—'

'Give me the car keys, Mum!'

'Freya, there's no way I'm letting you run through Cambridge on your own—'

'Give *me* the car keys,' a man's voice says firmly, cutting through my frantic babbling. 'I'll go.'

I turn to face him. He's tall and thin, with floppy, straight, dark brown hair and brown eyes, but I don't notice any of that at first. I'm too busy staring at his bike.

If only I had a bike right now . . . But no, that

4

still wouldn't work. I couldn't leave Freya alone in the centre of Cambridge. If she were just a few years older . . . but she isn't. She's nine.

'Obviously, I kind of overheard,' says the dark-haired man. 'As did all of Cambridge, and indeed most of England.' He smiles to let me know he's teasing me in a friendly way. 'Where have you parked, and where are you headed? I'll get the music there in time or die trying.' He makes an over-the-top comic 'death-throes' face at Freya, who looks up at me hopefully.

'Never trust a stranger,' the man tells her solemnly. 'Apart from when you've got an important audition – right, young lady?'

'Right,' Freya agrees, and I'm startled by the passion in her voice.

There is a group of about ten people standing nearby staring at us – watching the drama unfold, wondering if I'll say yes or no. Why do they care? It's not a marriage proposal, for God's sake.

My head fills with a muddled jumble of words: *only chance . . . bike . . . fast . . . yes, that'll work . . . he seems nice . . . could be anyone . . . might steal car.*

Instead of giving him my keys, I could ask to borrow his bike. I'd have to ask him to wait with Freya, though, and I can't do that. I'd sooner risk my Volvo than my child.

As if he can read my mind, the man says, 'I'll be quicker than you. I'm a cycling superstar, the Lance Armstrong of Cambridge. Actually, these days I'm probably faster. Since he gave up drugs, poor old Lance can barely wheel his bike as far as the post office without sweating and wheezing.'

I can't help smiling at his absurd joke. Offhand, I can't remember when anyone – friend, relative or stranger – has tried so hard to make me laugh and, at the same time, solve a problem for me.

He holds out his hand for my car keys.

I give them to him. A voice in my head whispers, 'Most people wouldn't do this,' but the whisper isn't loud enough to stop me.

Sod it. He's our only hope of getting Freya's sheet music to the audition on time. Whatever happens – even if this stranger steals my battered old Volvo and I never see him or it again – Freya will know that I did everything I could. That I took a risk to help her.

'Nice one, Mum,' she breathes. Her smile tells me I've made the right choice. Not perhaps the most sensible choice, but the right one.

'Grand Arcade car park, level 2,' I say too fast. My words trip over themselves. Even with a bike on our side, we can't afford to waste a second. 'Silver Volvo S60, MM02 OXY. On the back seat there's some sheet music for a song, "The Ash Grove".'

'And I'm bringing it to . . .?'

'Brooking Hall, next to—'

'I know it.' He mounts his bike, winks at Freya and cycles away at speed. Dangerously fast. Maybe he wasn't kidding when he said he'd die trying. I watch him disappear, his black overcoat flying out behind him like a cape – the kind a superhero might wear.

'Come on, Mum!' Freya grabs my arm and starts to drag me along the street. Before too long, annoyed by my slowness, she drops my sleeve and marches on ahead.

I hurry to catch up with her, stunned by what I've just done. I've given my car keys to a man I don't know at all. What kind of crazy fool am I? I didn't even ask his name, didn't get his mobile phone number . . . What will Lorna say when I tell her?

I know exactly what she'll say. She might be my oldest and most loyal friend, but she also enjoys insulting me when she thinks I deserve it.

'This is typical of you, Chloe,' she'll sigh. 'You're so dumb! Why would a total stranger put himself out to help you? You deserve to have your car nicked.'

'Darling, don't get your hopes up, okay?' I pant at Freya, out of breath from walking too fast. 'He might not get there in time. He might not turn up at all.'

'Yes, he will,' she insists. 'Stop being so negative!'

We arrive at the hall with one minute to spare. A woman with greasy skin and a hole in her tights snaps in my face, 'I'm sorry, we're running late.' She's carrying a brown clipboard under her arm. There are chunks missing out of its side, as if it's been nibbled by an animal.

Running late. I let the words sink in. Of course: we're not allowed to be late, but they – the people with all the power – can keep us hanging around as long as they like.

No need for all my panic. No need to hand over my car keys to a total stranger.

'Sit over there,' Clipboard Woman barks at me, pointing to a row of chairs that other people are already sitting in. She doesn't even look at Freya. 'We'll call your name when we're ready for you. I'm SORRY, we're running late . . .' she snarls at the mother and son who have just walked in behind us. They both flinch. Is there any need for her to bellow at people?

Still. Thank God for this delay. The man with the bike is not here yet.

Of course he isn't, fool. He'll be halfway to London by now – cruising along the motorway in your Volvo, laughing his head off at your stupidity.

'This is ridiculous,' a tired-looking bald man says to the girl sitting next to him. I assume she's his daughter. She has serious braces on her teeth. They look painful. 'You were supposed to be in a half hour ago. I'm not spending the whole day sat here.'

I look at my watch. Eleven thirty-two. Freya's audition was meant to start two minutes ago. I also don't want to wait for ever. On the other hand, I would like to get my car keys back.

If he were planning to bring them back, he'd be here by now . . .

I hear singing in the distance. Then louder, closer. Not a child's voice, though – a man's, coming from behind me. I know the song painfully well: 'The Ash Grove'. Freya's audition song, the one she's been practising for so long.

'Down yonder green valley where
    streamlets meander,
When twilight is fading, I pensively
    rove . . .'

I spin round. It's him. *Thank you, Lord.* He's singing at me, with a wide grin on his face.

9

It's a bit embarrassing in front of all these people.

I want to text Lorna to report that a handsome stranger is singing to me in public. I know what she'd text back: 'Pictures or it didn't happen.' She always demands proof of everything – photographic proof, ideally.

Freya gets to the point. 'Did you get my music?' she asks.

The dark-haired man matches her solemn face with his own as he hands over the sheets of paper. 'Job done, Your Highness. I pensively roved, I got your music. I even locked the car, so no need to worry about local vagrants hosting a party in it. That happened to my friend Keiran a couple of weeks ago. He came back to find empty cider bottles and burger wrappers all over the back seat of his hundred-grand BMW. He was not amused. So . . . what are you auditioning *for*?' our rescuer asks Freya. 'I hope it's going to make you a superstar, whatever it is.'

'Thank you *so* much,' I say, finding my voice at last. I must stop staring at him like someone who has seen a strange vision. I still can't quite believe he did this huge favour for us, with no other motive. He honestly wanted to help. Is anybody really so kind and selfless?

'She's auditioning to be one of the chorus in *Joseph and His Dreamcoat*,' I say. 'But that's only thanks to your help. If it weren't for you, we'd be trudging home in tears right now, so . . . thank you. I can't tell you how grateful I am.'

I'm in danger of crying. How silly. Anyone would think no one had ever been kind to me before. I blink frantically.

'You're welcome, ma'am.'

Ma'am?

Right. That's the worst fake American accent I've ever heard. And . . . oh, my God, now he's saluting me.

'*Joseph and His Dreamcoat*?' he says, frowning. 'Last I heard, it was called *Joseph and His Amazing Technicolour Dreamcoat*. Have they dropped the Amazing Technicolour part?'

'No,' I tell him. 'I just couldn't be bothered to say it.'

'What a rebel you are. While you're at it, there are probably some words in the musical itself that could do with a trim. I saw it when I was a teenager – at the Palace Theatre in Manchester, my home town. I still remember the words of the song about Pharaoh: "No one had rights or a vote but the king./In fact you might say he was *fairly right-wing*." Awful, just awful!'

He sounds very jolly about it, as if awfulness is one of his favourite things.

'The tunes are brilliant,' says Freya. 'It's a musical. The music's more important than the words.'

'I'm not sure I'd agree, Your Highness. When the words are *that* bad . . . Still, only one thing really matters, and that's launching your career as one of the great divas of our time. Am I right?'

'Um . . .' Freya looks at me, unsure what to say.

'And why aim to be in the chorus?' our new friend goes on. 'You should be going for the main part.'

'The main part's Joseph,' says Freya, sounding a little impatient. 'I'm a girl.'

'Well, girl or not, I think you'd make a great Joseph. Or a great Technicolour Dreamcoat – one or the other. And don't dare to tell me you're not a coat! Enough of this modesty!'

Freya laughs and blushes. I laugh too. I can't help it.

'Okay, ladies, well . . . I'd better be on my way. Knock 'em dead. Here are your car keys. Oh, hold on . . .'

Instead of my keys, he pulls an iPhone out of his pocket. It's ringing. His ringtone is 'The

Real Slim Shady' by Eminem, which surprises me. He's wearing a smart grey suit, with red bicycle clips around the bottoms of his trousers. Not a man who looks as if he'd be into rap music.

He glances at his phone, then puts it to his ear. 'Tom Rigby,' he says.

Tom Rigby. Tom Rigby. I'm glad I know his name, though I'm not sure why. He's a stranger. In a minute he's going to walk out of here and I'll never see him again.

He's talking about his work. It makes no sense to me. Something about chips and a database. I don't think he means the kind of chips you put salt and vinegar on.

He keeps saying a name: Camiga, or Camigo. Perhaps it's a company name. It sounds like the kind of thing a large, serious company might call itself. Very different from my own tiny business, Danglies – but then I work alone, make earrings and earn hardly any money.

When he's finished talking, Tom Rigby stuffs his phone back into his pocket and pulls out my car keys. His hand touches mine as he passes them to me. 'There you go,' he says. 'Right, I've got to scoot. Best of luck, Freya.'

He must have heard me saying her name when we were shouting on Bridge Street. His tone has changed from teasing to plain and direct. Obviously he has finished joking around and wants to get on with the rest of his day.

Which is fair enough.

'Thank you again!' I call after him as he walks away.

2

'Chloe, for God's sake! Freya's a talented singer – of course she got in! Do you think this Tom Rigby bloke's got magic powers? He hasn't. He's just a charming, handsome man with red bicycle clips. This is Freya's success, not his.'

It is a week after the *Joseph* auditions. I'm in The Eagle pub on Benet Street, having a drink with my best friend and harshest critic, Lorna Tams. Lorna is forty-two, ten years older than me. Two years ago, she left her husband, Josh. She has since divorced him, and come up with a line to describe him: 'A nice enough bloke, but not the husband I deserve.'

When I first met Lorna, she worked in a brewery. Now's she's given that up and is training to be a Methodist minister. When I asked her about the change of career, she said, 'Beer got boring.'

I know nothing about the Methodist church. I hope they like their ministers to wear low-cut tops and sneer, or else Lorna won't fit in at all.

'Tom Rigby didn't cast a spell that made the judges say yes to Freya,' she says now. 'He did you a favour for sure, but he isn't some kind of . . . good luck charm on legs.'

Then why do I feel as if that's exactly what he is?

'A hundred and twenty-three children auditioned for the chorus,' I tell Lorna. 'Only twenty got in. Freya was one of them. I'm not saying it was down to Tom Rigby alone, but . . . there *was* something magical about him turning up.'

'Magical? You mean you fancied him?'

'No, I didn't,' I say crossly. 'I didn't think about him in that way at all.'

'Hmm.' Lorna narrows her eyes. 'All right, then. So we're going to stop talking about him, are we, and talk about your talented daughter instead?'

I bite my lip. Sometimes I wish Lorna weren't as clever as she is. It would make my life a whole lot easier.

The truth is, I am not quite ready to forget all about Tom Rigby.

'I need to thank him,' I say quietly – so quietly that I can hardly hear my own words over the louder voices of the students at the table next to ours. I don't like this part of The Eagle. I would prefer to sit in the room to the right of the front door, which is less noisy, but Lorna always insists on sitting in what she calls 'the historical part'.

'You did thank him,' she points out, like a policeman trying to pick holes in a suspect's story. 'Several times, from what you've told me.'

'I *said* thank you, yes, but I'd like to thank him properly. He did us such a huge favour.'

'Right. By "thank him properly", you of course mean hunt him down and force him to marry you?'

'No, I mean I'd like to get him a card, or—' I daren't finish my sentence. I stare down at the table, too embarrassed to say any more.

'A card *or*?' Lorna laughs. 'It's so easy to see through you! A card *or*,' she repeats. 'You've already got him a present, haven't you? What? Tell me! What did you buy him? Ugh, Chloe, I despair of you. Have you bought anything for your star of a daughter, by the way? The one who actually, y'know, got the part in *Joseph*?'

'Yes. I made her something.'

I don't feel like telling Lorna that the 'something' was a necklace: a little glass box on a chain, with a tiny technicolour dreamcoat inside it. It took me four whole days to get it right. It's beautiful, and Freya loves it. If Lorna wants to think I'm ignoring my daughter in

17

favour of a handsome stranger, let her. It will serve her right to be wrong.

'And what did you make for Tom Rigby?' she asks, eyeing me warily.

I feel my face heat up. My present for Tom only took me half a day to make. It was much less fiddly: a tie-pin. Musical notes inside a metal frame. Notes from 'The Ash Grove', Freya's audition song.

Down yonder green valley where streamlets meander . . .

'You're too embarrassed to tell me what you've made for him,' says Lorna, watching me closely. 'This does not bode well. Is it a dildo covered in love hearts?'

I can't be bothered to reply to this insulting suggestion.

'How can you give it to him, anyway? You don't know where to find him.'

'I can try. I heard him say the name of a company, when he was talking on his phone. Camigo, or Camiga. Maybe that's where he works. It should be easy enough to find.'

Lorna groans into her pint of ginger beer shandy. 'You're serious about this, aren't you? You're planning to track him down. Don't. Listen to me, Chloe.'

'Do I have a choice?'

'Tom Rigby came to your and Freya's rescue when you needed it. He was your saviour for twenty minutes one Saturday morning. But the moment has passed, as all moments do. You thanked him, and now it's over. You're back to being strangers.'

Lorna has more to say. She always does. 'All this making him presents and trying to find him, it's not about thanking him properly. Can't you see that? You're craving a repeat performance – more of his magic. You want him to save you again. Maybe for longer this time, right? Maybe for ever.'

'Lorna, I don't want to marry Tom Rigby. I don't even know him.'

'You want to get to know him,' she says.

If I did, would it be a crime?

'No, I don't,' I say. 'Look, I just don't want to let him disappear with no more than a "Thank you so much" from me. I want to put myself out for him, like he put himself out for me and Freya. So, yes, I've made him a present,' I say defiantly. 'Not because I want him to scoop me up and ride off into the sunset with me, but purely for the sake of doing a nice, generous thing. What's so wrong with that?'

Lorna shakes her head. 'You know what? Part of my issue is that this guy sounds too nice.

"Ma'am"? "Your Highness"? I mean, yuck! Okay, so he didn't steal your car – and who can blame him? That Volvo's a rusty old heap of junk – but what if the whole "Look, I'm giving you back your car keys" thing was a trick to reel you in?'

This idea is so stupid, it makes me laugh. 'Well, then he failed, didn't he?' I say. 'Like you said: as far as he knows, he's never going to see me again. And why on earth would he want to "reel me" anywhere? You think he took one look at me screaming at Freya on Bridge Street and thought, "That woman looks well-heeled. I'm going to come to her rescue, charm her into marrying me, then murder her and inherit her savings that are worth all of a thousand pounds"?'

'That's true.' Lorna stares at me. It's clear she disapproves of what she sees. 'You definitely don't look as if you've got anything worth inheriting. All right, I'll be blunt. Blunt*er*, I should say. I'm wary of Tom Rigby for one reason only: because you're not. Don't be offended, Chloe, but you're a *terrible* judge of character.'

'And you're my best friend. So if you're right, what does that say about you?' I sigh. 'Is it really so terrible that he called me "Ma'am" and Freya "Your Highness"?'

'No,' Lorna says after a pause. 'You're right. We have no reason to think Tom Rigby is anything but lovely.'

Then she leans both her elbows on the table and glares at me. 'That's why he doesn't deserve to be psycho-stalked by you. He did you a favour – great! – and then he said goodbye and walked away. Did he ask for your number? No. Did he suggest meeting again? No. So give the poor man a break and *leave him alone*, Chloe.'

3

'Useless Google!' I mutter at my computer screen later that night. It's nearly one o'clock in the morning. I really ought to get some sleep, but I'm too stubborn. I refuse to go to bed defeated. And since Freya is at my mum's until lunchtime tomorrow, it's the perfect chance for me to do some research.

I can't find any company called Camigo or Camiga that looks as if Tom Rigby might work for it. There's Camigo Media, but they make games apps for mobile phones. I'm pretty sure that wasn't what Tom's business call was about. He was discussing a bank, I think. He didn't say the word 'bank', but I got the idea that he worked with money.

The only Tom Rigbys and Thomas Rigbys in Cambridge that I've managed to find online are definitely not him. One is too old. Another has the wrong face in his LinkedIn photo.

Where do I go from here? What else can I

search for? 'Tom Rigby red bicycle clips'? 'Tom Rigby sings "The Ash Grove"'?

Absurd.

I type 'Dr T Rigby' into the internet search box and find a Dr Thomas Rigby in the United States who is an expert in crop science. He's not the man I'm looking for, and so, for a moment, I hate him.

I'm never going to find my Tom Rigby. Why is that such a terrible prospect? There must be something wrong with me. Lorna was right. I must be crazier than even she suspects, to allow a complete and utter stranger to become so important to me.

A horrible thought crosses my mind: what if that's not his name? What if he was talking about somebody else called Tom Rigby, and I got it wrong?

No, that's impossible. He said it in a 'My name is . . .' kind of way, just after he answered the phone. I was sure at the time.

My phone buzzes on the table next to me, making me jump. It's Lorna. She has texted, 'Don't Google him!'

I text back, 'I can't find him anyway.'

'Really?' she replies. 'I found him in 30 secs. Which I know I should not tell you!'

I grab my phone and ring her, my hands shaking. This had better not be a joke.

I wait and wait. *Come on, Lorna. I know your phone's in your hand.*

When she finally picks it up, she says dryly, 'My desire to show off was stronger than my wish to protect you from making a tit of yourself. What can I say? I'm a flawed human being.'

'Tell me,' I say.

She sighs. 'Draw breath first, and let's go over the pros and cons. Chloe, I really think—'

'Tell me!'

'Will you listen to the desperation in your voice?'

'Yeah – my desperation not to be toyed with by my sadistic so-called friend. You have the information I want, and you're dangling it in front of me like bait. Stop dicking around and *tell me*, so that I can go to bed.'

'Ha! Like you're going to put your pyjamas on and drift off to the Land of Nod as soon as you know. Bollocks! You'll be up all night Googling this guy – just as soon as I've told you who he is.'

'Lorna—'

'All right, give me a chance! His name isn't Tom Rigby, R-I-G-B-Y. It's Tom Rigbey with an "e". R-I-G-B-*E*-Y. He's the CSO of a company

24

called CamEgo – one word, capital C, capital E, ego as in egotist. Now let me try to describe what they do without falling asleep. It sounds so dull. They design software that helps with payment compliance in the financial sector, worldwide. Before you ask, I haven't a clue what that means.'

'But CSO, that's—'

'Car Keys and Songs Officer,' Lorna fires back.

'Chief something, isn't it?'

'Chief Science Officer. He's a smart cookie, is Tom Rigbey.'

I frown. That's strange. He didn't look like a boss or manager of anything. He looked too young, for a start – about my age, mid-thirties. And . . . wouldn't a Chief Science Officer need to behave more sensibly in public places?

'Chloe? Do *not* go to CamEgo's offices and ambush him. And – since you'll ignore that – ring me as soon as you have. I want all the details.'

4

I arrive at CamEgo's offices at nine o'clock sharp on Monday morning – probably before most of the firm's employees. The office building is as glossy and shiny as I imagined it would be. It's one of the newly built ones on Brooklands Avenue, close to the Botanic Gardens. CamEgo has the top three floors, and I'm waiting on the lowest of these, in reception.

There are two women behind the desk, one in her late fifties and the other in her early twenties. Both are wearing white blouses, black skirts, and CamEgo badges with their names on. Should I approach Nadine Caspian, the younger woman, or Rukia Yunis, if I have a choice? Both are dealing with other people. I hope one finishes before the other, so that I don't have to choose.

I've worked out what I'll say. I don't want or need to see Tom Rigbey – that would be too awkward and embarrassing – so I'll simply ask if I can leave the gift bag I've brought, and will they make sure to deliver it safely to him?

As well as the hand-made tie-pin, I've written a note and put it in the bag. It's short and to the point: 'Thank you for the music (as ABBA might say!) Lots of love, Chloe (and Freya, who got into *Joseph* thanks to you!)' No kisses. Though I couldn't resist writing my email address in the top right hand corner.

The ABBA joke is not something I'd have put in a note to anyone else, and I'm not sure if it's witty or just annoying. I included it because it popped into my head and struck me as the kind of silly quip Tom Rigbey might enjoy.

In my first draft of the note, I pointed out the musical content of the tie-pin and told him the notes came from 'The Ash Grove'. I wanted to make sure he'd notice. Then, later, I decided it was crass to point it out. So I tore up what I'd written and started again.

Tom will work it out. Chief Science Officers are clever.

The receptionist called Nadine Caspian is free, having sent the man she was dealing with to wait on a red sofa to her left. 'Can I help you?' She smiles at me. 'Ooh – have you brought me a prezzie? And it isn't even my birthday!'

I make a noise that sounds like laughing, and hope my ABBA joke is less feeble than that. People who aren't funny shouldn't try to be.

Is that what Tom Rigbey will think when he reads my note?

'It is a present, but I'm afraid it's not for you,' I say.

'Ah, well – never mind!' She chuckles. 'At least you've left the bag open, so I can have a nosey at it.' She peers in. 'Hm, a jewellery box. Let me guess: cufflinks for the man in your life?'

That's strange. I was going to make cufflinks – that was my first idea, before I decided a tie-pin would be better. Cufflinks seemed too obvious.

If Lorna were here she would tell Nadine Caspian that the contents of the box in the bag were none of her business. One of her favourite rants is about people who, under cover of friendliness, poke their noses into your affairs in an unacceptable way. This includes hotel receptionists who say while checking you in, 'So, any special plans for this evening, then?' (To which Lorna once replied with a straight face, 'Yes, as a matter of fact: I'm meeting my lover and we're going to try anal sex for the first time. Is that the kind of special plan you mean?')

I'm not as brave or outrageous as Lorna. Even so, I won't answer Nadine Caspian's question.

Instead I say, 'It's for Tom Rigbey. I believe he works here?'

Nadine's face twitches. She swallows hard. 'Tom Rigbey?' Her friendly, open manner of a second ago is gone. I heard alarm in her voice when she said his name. Now she's looking at me warily.

'Yes. Isn't he CSO here?' I ask.

Nadine nods. 'He's out all day today. London.' These are the words I hear, but the message is clear: 'Go away. Get lost.'

'That's fine,' I say. 'I don't need to see him. I just wanted to leave this for him.'

The other receptionist, Rukia Yunis, who is now free and listening to us, leans over and says, 'Of course. That's no problem at all. If you give it to me, I'll see that Tom gets it.'

Our eyes meet and I see an apology in hers: *I'm sorry my colleague is acting like an arse.*

I hand her the gift bag, thank her, and turn to leave, wondering if Nadine Caspian is in love with Tom Rigbey. Probably. That would explain her sudden shift from far-too-matey to cold and hostile. She must think I'm some kind of girlfriend. Maybe *she's* his girlfriend, and thinks I'm trying to steal him away.

I'm halfway down the stairs to the floor below when I hear a voice behind me. 'Hey! Wait.'

I turn. It's her: Nadine. 'Sorry if I was a bit off just then,' she says.

'It's fine.'

'Well, not really. It's not your fault. I just . . .' She sighs. 'There you were with a present, and it turns out to be for Tom Rigbey of all people . . .'

I nearly open my mouth to ask, 'What do you mean "of all people"?' Something stops me. I'm not sure I want to hear the answer she'd give. I haven't chosen to have this chat. Nadine Caspian followed me. Forced it on me.

She's standing three steps above me on the staircase. It makes me feel trapped and small. I wish we could talk on the same level, but we can hardly stand side by side on one step – they're too narrow.

I can't decide if she's attractive or not. Her hair is nice: dark blonde, thick and subtly high-lighted. Her face is heart-shaped and her features big and doll-like, but with a slightly hardened look to them. She looks as if she's in her mid to late twenties.

'Something tells me you haven't known Tom Rigbey long,' she says. 'You don't know him well – am I right?'

I nod.

'This is none of my business, but I'll say it anyway. You seem like a lovely person, so go and get your gift bag back off Rukia and give it to someone else, *anyone* else. Have nothing to do with Tom Rigbey. Give him nothing, tell him nothing, trust him not at all. Avoid him like the plague because that's what he is – a plague in human form.'

I can hardly breathe. Did she really just say that? All I can hear is my too-loud heartbeat, as if it's bouncing off the narrow walls of the stairwell.

'And no, he hasn't just dumped me, if that's what you're thinking,' Nadine adds. 'He's the CSO of the company I work for – I have no personal connection to him – but . . . I know how dangerous he is.'

When I find my voice, I say, 'Dangerous how?'

'Are you going to take my advice?' Nadine responds with a question. 'Are you going to get that gift bag back?'

'I . . . I haven't decided.'

'Then I can't talk to you. If you're under his spell, you'll tell him anything I say. Tomorrow morning I'll find myself out of a job.'

'No, I . . .' I stop myself because I might. I

31

might tell Tom Rigbey that one of his receptionists is a nosey troublemaker with no respect
for other people's privacy. I liked him, and I
don't like Nadine Caspian. 'I can't promise
anything without knowing what you're talking
about,' I say.

Am I being stupid? If there's a side of Tom
Rigbey that I need to be warned about, I should
find out what it is. I try again. 'Can you please
tell me what you mean?'

She shakes her head. 'Sorry. Look, it's your
life, and none of my business. I should keep
my mouth shut. Please don't tell him I said
anything and . . . please forget I did.' She looks
and sounds scared as she pushes past me and
hurries down the stairs. I expected her to go
back up to CamEgo's reception, but perhaps
she needs to go out and wouldn't have followed
me otherwise.

Not telling Tom Rigbey what she said,
assuming I ever meet him again, will be easy.
It was so horrible. So extreme. Surely unde-
served, too. How could anyone apart from the
worst, most evil criminals deserve to be spoken
of like that? Repeating such nasty insults to a
man who has only ever been kind to me . . .
it's unthinkable. He'd be so hurt.

Forgetting what's just happened is going to

be slightly harder. If Nadine Caspian wanted me to forget, she should have chosen words that wouldn't sit so heavily in my mind.

'Give him nothing, tell him nothing, trust him not at all. Avoid him like the plague because that's what he is – a plague in human form.'

5

'So what did you do?' Lorna is fizzing with excitement.

I've left Freya with my mum, and Lorna and I are in St John's Chop House having dinner. Several hours have passed since my exchange with Nadine Caspian. I still haven't forgotten what she said.

'I—'

'No, wait, don't tell me. I want to guess.' Lorna shovels a forkful of mashed potatoes into her mouth. 'You hung around on the stairs for nearly an hour, worrying about whether to leave the present where it was or go and get it back. In the end you decided to leave it. Right?'

'No. I went back to reception and asked the other receptionist, Rukia, to give me back the gift bag—'

'Really? Wow, well done!'

'Wait. I didn't take the present away. I just tore the top off my note – the part where I'd put my contact details. I thought that was the perfect compromise: Tom Rigbey gets his thank-you present, which he deserves and which I want him to have, but I haven't given him my email address. So, if this Nadine woman's right and he's dangerous . . . well, he's no danger to me, is he? He has no way of getting in touch.'

Lorna sighs. 'It's a compromise,' she says. 'I'm not sure I'd call it perfect. You really took the gift bag back, tore the top off your note, then stuck it back in the bag and gave it back to the receptionist?'

'Yes.'

'She must have thought you were a nutter.'

'You don't think I did the right thing?'

Lorna snorts. 'Don't look so sad. I never think you do the right thing. You're way too soft and soppy about people.'

'What would you have done?'

'First off, I'd have sworn on my honour not to breathe a word of what Nadine told me to Tom Rigbey – that way you might have found something out. But even based only on what she said to you, I'd have asked for my prezzie back and fled, thankful for a useful warning and a narrow escape.'

I stare at my pasta with wild mushrooms, wondering how long it will be before Lorna orders me to eat it. Will I admit to having lost

35

my appetite, or force it down just to shut her up?

'I know what you're thinking, Chloe: "Mean, nasty Lorna, not giving Tom Rigbey the benefit of the doubt. What if Nadine is wrong? Wouldn't it be unfair to think badly of Tom Rigbey with no evidence at all – just hearsay, just someone's opinion?"'

'Yes. Pretty much, that is what I'm thinking,' I say.

'You think I'm saying, "There's no smoke without fire," that rumours don't start for no reason, so there must be some grain of truth in it?' Lorna pauses to take a gulp of red wine. 'I'm not saying that, though. Sometimes there *is* smoke without fire – anyone with a brain knows that – so you have to ask yourself: what kind of smoke is it? If Nadine had said, "You don't want to get involved with Tom Rigbey – he's a womaniser and a heart-breaker" or something like that, you could safely ignore her. That kind of thing can mean anything. It'd most likely mean he turned down her advances. But "a plague in human form"? "Give him nothing, tell him nothing . . ."? And you said she looked scared? Chloe, come on – that's got to be a warning worth listening to.'

'So, because she said really terrible things

about him, that means she can't be wrong? Why?'

Lorna groans. 'How are we still friends?'

'I've no idea.' I put my fork in my mouth, to create the illusion of eating. I can't imagine being hungry any time soon.

'This isn't a court of law, Chloe. Would Nadine's warning be enough to get Tom Rigbey locked up for ever? No, and nor should it be. It's just gossip. But she works with him. She knows him. You don't. He can't matter to you that much – a man you've spoken to only once? If a stranger warns you to steer clear because he's a plague person, why wouldn't you listen to them? Nadine could be wrong, I'm not denying that, but isn't it much more likely that she's right?'

Lorna's questions have stopped sounding like questions, because they aren't. They're opinions, put in question form for effect. That's why, even though I have answers to each and every one, I don't feel like sharing them with her.

It's not true that Tom Rigbey can't matter to me that much. He does. I only met him once, but that one time filled me with hope. Hope for what, though? Nothing will happen. Nothing can. I tore my email address off the note. He can't contact me, even if he wants to.

Perhaps I ought to try to believe Nadine Caspian, to make myself feel better. If I can get myself to believe I've had a narrow escape . . .

'And, great, now you're not eating.' Lorna throws up her hands. 'Going off your food because Nadine the receptionist might have unfairly slagged off your favourite stranger makes no sense, Chloe. You're living in a fantasy world. Whatever your instincts are telling you right now, for God's sake do the opposite. Your judgement's completely messed up.'

'We don't need to talk about it any more,' I say quietly.

'Good. Fantastic.'

'He hasn't got my email or phone number. So: end of story.'

'Praise the Lord!'

'You're forgetting that I've actually met him. I'm not weighing Nadine's bitching against nothing, I'm weighing it against my own first-hand experience. Tom Rigbey did something amazing for me and Freya, something no one else would have done. I spoke to him. We chatted. I just don't believe her!'

'Right. Because no evil maniacs know how to chat nicely and fool people. If someone can make a few witty comments about an Andrew

Lloyd Webber musical, that proves they're a good person.'

'So now you're making out he's a psychopath?' I snap.

'You know what, Chloe? I *do* believe Nadine. I don't think people say things like that for no reason. I haven't got any proof, but I don't like the sound of Tom Rigbey. Didn't from your first mention of him. All this "Ma'am" and "Your Highness" stuff, saluting you, cycling off to the car park for Freya's music as if someone's life depended on it . . . It's too much. Way too much.

'You said it yourself,' Lorna goes on. '"He did something no one else would have done". And you didn't ask him to, did you? He overheard, and forced his way in. There was your alarm bell, right there.You chose to see it in a positive light because you're naïve, but if you ask me, it's creepy.'

'You could be right,' I say, not caring if I mean it or not. A lot of my chats with Lorna end this way. She loves arguing and could go on all night. I hate it, and usually give in.

I wish I hadn't taken the note out of the gift bag and torn the top off it. I let a stranger scare me off. If I'd taken no notice of her, I would now be looking forward to hearing from Tom

Rigbey. He'd have emailed and thanked me. He might have said something about the present and how much he liked it. Whatever he'd have written, I bet it would have made me laugh. Lorna's always telling me that she has my best interests at heart, but most of what she says makes me feel worse, not better.

I wish I'd argued with Nadine Caspian. Tom Rigbey is not a plague in human form. No way. That's too over the top. I don't buy it. He's sweet, and not dangerous at all. I trusted him with my car keys, and he didn't let me down. I'm the one who's let him down by letting myself be scared away by the spiteful words of a stranger.

And now I'll never hear from him again.

6

Except – and thank you, life, for being so surprising and almost making me believe in God – I do hear from Tom Rigbey again, and in a pleasingly familiar way.

Four days after my depressing dinner with Lorna, I'm sitting on a bench on Castle Street, waiting for Freya to come out of her first *Joseph* rehearsal, when I hear a man's voice singing a song:

'Down yonder green valley, where
    streamlets meander,
When twilight is fading, I pensively
    rove.
Or at the bright noontide in solitude
    wander,
Amid the dark shades of the lonely ash
    grove;
Twas there, while the blackbird was
    cheerfully singing . . .'

It's him. I leap to my feet. 'Tom Rigbey!' Oops. That was uncool. Too late now to pretend I'm not thrilled to see him. He's got his bike with him. Same red bicycle clips as last time, a black suit, white shirt with thin blue and lilac stripes . . .

'Hello, Chloe Whose-Surname-I-Still-Don't-Know-Because-She-Didn't-Write-It-On-Her-Card.' He sounds equally thrilled to see me. My heart is bouncing up and down like an excited toddler in a soft play centre ball pit.

'This is . . . such a surprise,' I stammer.

'I hunted you down. I'm as ruthless as I am cunning, you see. You don't mind, do you?'

He is obviously joking. I am obviously not going to mention to Lorna that he described himself as ruthless and cunning.

He says, 'You wrote in your note that Freya got a part in the play. I found out where and when the rehearsals were. I knew you'd be exactly where I've found you, waiting to collect your talented daughter.'

'You were right. Here I am!'

'They don't call me The Talented Mr Rigbey for nothing. Now, may I show you this beautiful tie-pin I'm wearing? With what I like to think of as "our song" . . .' – he mimes quote marks in the air – '"The Ash Grove" contained within

42

it! What an incredibly thoughtful idea. I *love* it. Seriously, I can't think of any present I've ever been given before that I've loved anywhere *near* as much. Where did you get it from? I'm guessing . . . the Folk Song Tie-Pins Warehouse, just off the M11, right?'

I giggle. 'I made it.'

'You *made* it? Wow. You're a genius, Chloe No-Surname.'

'No, I'm not. I'm a jewellery maker – that's what I do. And I'm Daniels.'

'Daniel's? Who is this Daniel? I'll have him killed.'

Another joke not to be repeated to Lorna. Though, actually, maybe I should tell her. No one who was planning to commit murder would announce it so cheerfully and openly.

'I mean my surname is Daniels. Chloe Daniels.'

'Oh. Well, that's a relief. I must admit, I was rather hoping you didn't belong to anybody – apart from Her Highness Freya, that is. But this jewellery business of yours sounds amazing. When did you start it up? What's it called? Is it just you, or do you have a whole team?'

Normally, I like to be asked about my work. It might be a trivial thing to spend my days doing, but I love it. I look forward to making each new piece, and not many people can say that about their work. And I love having a company, however tiny. I loved choosing its name, all by myself, not having to consult anyone else.

'It's called Danglies,' I say. I can't manage any more words at the moment. My brain is busy, bouncing around the idea that Tom Rigbey doesn't want me to belong to anyone. He definitely said that – I didn't imagine it – and there's only one thing it can mean.

'Ah, *voilà Mademoiselle Freya!*' Tom exclaims, as she comes out of the rehearsal hall and runs towards us. I don't speak French, but I'm guessing that he said something like, 'Here comes the lovely Freya'.

'Well done for getting a part, young lady. Have you been made Pharaoh yet? I'm sure it won't be long.'

'What are you doing here?' Freya asks him.

'I wanted to thank your mother for the present she made for me, and she annoyingly didn't give me her phone number, hoping to shake me off. So I've had to become a musical theatre groupie.'

'I wasn't hoping that at all,' I say. 'I didn't want you to think I expected a thank you, that's all.'

I've just lied to Tom Rigbey. Nadine Caspian warned me that he was not to be trusted. Maybe she should have warned him about me. So far in the very short time we've known each other, he's been nothing but lovely to me and I've failed him twice. Once by taking Nadine's stupid badmouthing too seriously, and now by lying to him.

'I wouldn't have thought that for a moment,' he says. 'And I'm not letting you off the hook, I'm afraid. I think, since you've put me out by making me roam the streets looking for you, I ought to be allowed to take you out for dinner very soon. You and Freya, if she'd like to come too.'

'Don't invite me.' Freya rolls her eyes. 'I mean, thanks, and I get what you're trying to do, but . . . it's silly. You should just invite Mum, on her own. I won't feel left out or anything like that.'

'Oh.' Tom frowns. 'Thanks for the tip. You really are a well-adjusted child. See, I feared that not inviting you might carry a hint of When-I-marry-your-mother-I-intend-to-keep-you-locked-in-the-cellar. Am I wrong? Because I totally wouldn't keep you locked in the cellar. I'm happy to shake on that now if you'd like?'

He extends his hand and Freya shakes it, smiling. She says, 'I love our cellar. It's where my Xbox is. I'd like to spend more time there.

In fact Mum's always dragging me upstairs to do dull, mind-improving things. Yawn.'

'You should always listen to your mother, if only because she runs a jewellery business and must have piles of diamonds.'

'That is *so* not true.' I laugh. 'My only experience of diamonds is seeing them in shop windows.'

'Then that must change,' says Tom Rigbey. 'Now, when can you lock your daughter in the cellar and have dinner with me?'

'What about tonight, Mum?' Freya suggests.

'Um. I'm not sure if—'

'Ninny'll babysit. You know she will. When does she ever say no?' To Tom, Freya says, 'That's my gran. Our WiFi's way faster than hers. She'd move in with us if she could.'

Tom bows. 'I greatly admire your tactical thinking, young lady. But we can't make plans unless your mother joins in with our plotting. What shall we do to persuade her? I mean, it's only dinner. It's not as if we're planning to blow up the Houses of Parliament.'

Freya laughs and tucks her hair behind her ear. She's clearly delighted to be treated as a key player. *Smart move, Talented Mr Rigbey.*

'All right,' I say. 'Dinner tonight.'

I'm glad this evening is still several hours

away. So much has been said during this short conversation that I need to think about. I want to make the arrangement as quickly as I can, so that I can escape from Tom.

I need to get away from him so that I can think about him properly, without him being there to distract me.

7

Tom and I meet for dinner at eight o'clock, at a restaurant called The Oak Bistro on Lensfield Road. I've never been here before, and it doesn't look like much from the outside, but inside it's beautiful. Striking, colourful paintings with price-tags attached cover whole walls. There are thick white tablecloths and proper napkins – or, as Tom said when we sat down at our table, 'None of your folded paper nonsense'. I notice there's an attractive outdoor eating area too, which must be fantastic in summer.

Will Tom and I ever sit out there? Will he still want to take me out for dinner by the time summer comes round?

Don't be an idiot, Chloe. Take it one day at a time.

I know why I'm feeling insecure, and I know how silly it is. Since we met this evening, Tom hasn't once mentioned marriage or diamonds. He seems to have two modes: playful and serious. Tonight he's in serious mode and not cracking daft jokes. He seems mainly to want to hear about my work and relationship history, and to tell me about his. Which is nice in a different way, but . . .

No. No buts. It's nice. I'm having a lovely time. It's just that after everything he said this afternoon, I was half expecting to arrive at The Oak Bistro and find him on one knee, holding out a diamond engagement ring, with an orchestra playing romantic music in the background.

I've read him wrong, clearly. He's not soppy and romantic. Thinking about it, he says some quite oddly unromantic things. A truly romantic person wouldn't joke about locking my daughter in the cellar.

Tom Rigbey is an unusual man. That doesn't mean he will never ask me to marry him. It's more likely to mean that, if he ever does, he will do it in an unusual way.

Not that I want to marry him, or would say yes. I barely know him.

I tell him about Freya's dad – my short relationship with him and our break-up. 'That sounds tough,' he says with feeling. Then, with a more mischievous expression on his face, he says, 'But your mother's been supportive, right? In exchange for great WiFi?'

I laugh. 'Actually . . . *now* she's great, and

Freya's right – she'll babysit whenever I need her to, but that's only since she split up with Husband Number 3. When I was on my own with a six-month-old baby, Mum had only just met Clive and was indulging his every need all day long. He was the child she looked after – and emotionally he was *such* a spoilt kid. She had no time for anyone else.'

'Could you ever indulge a Clive?' Tom wrinkles his nose. 'I couldn't. Names are important. I could indulge a Chloe, but never a Clive.'

I want to hear more about his one and only serious relationship. It was with a woman called Maddy, but he didn't have much to say about her. He moved on quite quickly once he'd told me they'd been together for four years, but split up when she'd moved to Australia for work. I'd feel nosey if I asked to know more.

I could ask about his parents instead. He hasn't mentioned them yet, and since we've just been discussing my mother . . . 'You said you grew up in Manchester. Are your folks still there?'

'Did I say that?' He frowns. 'When?'

'The first time we met. You mentioned the Palace Theatre, where you saw *Joseph Dreamcoat*.'

'There's going to be nothing left of that title by the time you finish with it, is there?' Tom chuckles. 'Remind me if I ever need to fake my own death and invent a new ID, Joseph Dreamcoat's my new name.

'You're quite right: I grew up in Manchester – and what a great memory you have! My brother Julian's still there. He's a dentist, in Fallowfield. My parents moved to Florida five years ago, in true retired-person style. I was sunbathing by their shared swimming pool a few months ago and saw what I thought was the most enormous upright lizard. It turned out to be an armadillo! I nearly freaked out, but managed to keep my cool for long enough to take a photo, which is now my Twitter avatar. When people ask why, I point out that the armadillo is far more handsome than I could ever hope to be. Okay, now I'm going to leave a gaping void in my chit-chat so that you can say, "Not at all, Tom – you are the sexiest man I've ever clapped eyes on."'

I smile. I might have said something – nothing nearly so extreme as his suggestion, but something in that direction – had he not made it so awkward for me to do so.

Our main courses arrive – fishcakes for me and steak for Tom – and we carry on chatting. By the end of the meal I know that he is not interested in politics, but plans to vote for

51

Nick Clegg in the next election because 'even though I have no clue what his policies are, he's been so savaged by the mob, I feel sorry for him.'

I learn, also, that Tom is fond of dogs (especially English Bull Terriers – as a child he had two, Butch and Sundance). He's also a keen chess player and a cinema addict. His favourite old movie is *What Ever Happened to Baby Jane?*, the Joan Crawford and Bette Davis classic, and his favourite new one is *Prisoners*, starring Hugh Jackman and Jake Gyllenhaal. I've seen the first but not the second.

I don't have a favourite film, and say so when asked. 'Then you'll need to get one, before the next time we meet,' Tom says. 'And please make sure it's not *Bridesmaids* or *Pretty Woman* or something revolting like that. Speaking of the next time we meet . . . I'd very much like to see you again. Are you free for dinner later in the week?'

'Who's Nadine Caspian?' I ask him. Shit. Why did I say that? Why? I can't tell Tom what she said – he'd be shocked and hurt. And I'd be a bitch for passing on bad gossip that probably has no basis whatsoever.

'Nadine?' He sounds and looks puzzled. 'She's a receptionist at my firm.'

'I know. I meant . . . is there anything between you and her?'

Tom's laugh suggests surprise more than amusement. 'Anything between me and Nadine? No. Not unless you mean the reception desk. I've said fewer than twenty words to her in my life.'

'I'm sorry – it's none of my business. Forget I asked.'

'Er, no. Why did you? Come on, what's going on? Why would you ask me if there was anything between me and a receptionist I barely notice from one day to the next?'

'I think I must have imagined it. When I gave her the present and asked her to make sure you got it, she looked sort of . . . odd. I just wondered if she might be a secret admirer, if not a girlfriend or ex.'

'Hm. I suppose it's possible she's a *very* secret admirer. She's never shown any interest in me. Now I come to think of it, she once showed no interest in a parcel I asked her to send. She didn't do it – she said she forgot.'

I feel a surge of excitement. This could be what I'm looking for.

'Did you tell her off for not sending the parcel?' A bollocking at work might be enough to make Nadine hate him.

Tom looks embarrassed. 'Actually, funny you should ask that. No, I didn't. I hate conflict. In fact I'm a real smoother-over by nature, so I made out Nadine had done exactly the right thing by not sending the parcel. I said I'd changed my mind and didn't want it to go out so soon after all, and silly old me for telling her it was urgent and needed to go straight away.'

'Oh.' There goes my theory.

'So what about dinner later in the week? I mean, tomorrow's probably too soon, is it? Especially for your mum, newly stocked up on WiFi as she is. Also – if I were you, I wouldn't want to see me again tomorrow. I'd be sick of me by now. And, actually, I have to go to London first thing tomorrow, so maybe I'll need longer than a day to—' He breaks off and smiles in a mysterious way. 'Sorry,' he says. 'Almost gave something away there. Oops – Tom the moron strikes again.'

'I'm not sick of you,' I tell him.

Don't agree to tomorrow. Make him wait at least a few days.

Why? What's the point?

What did he nearly give away? The sooner I see him again, the sooner I'll find out.

'Tomorrow's fine for me if it works for you,' I say.

8

'I need to speak to Nadine Caspian,' I say to Rukia Yunis, the receptionist who passed on my 'Ash Grove' tie-pin to Tom. Because she did this, I think of her as trustworthy. Perhaps that's crazy.

It's nine o'clock in the morning, the day after my dinner with Tom; also the day of my next dinner with Tom. I persuaded my mum to stay overnight. When she asked why I needed her to take Freya to school today, I mumbled something about getting my car to the garage early, then set off in my Volvo – the old, knackered one that Tom Rigbey missed his chance to steal – to CamEgo's offices.

Tom said he had to go to London first thing today, so it's the perfect time. Now or never, I decided. I plumped for now. If Tom turns up at La Mimosa this evening with a diamond ring and a marriage proposal – which of course he won't, but it's just possible – I will need not to have a head full of doubts and fears planted by Nadine Caspian. I'd like to sort this out once and for all, so that I can stop thinking about it.

'Nadine?' says Rukia Yunis doubtfully.

'Yes. She's a receptionist here. You were sitting next to—'

'I know who she is. She . . . she doesn't work here any more.'

'What?'

'I'm as surprised as you are,' Rukia says. 'I've just this second opened the email announcement.'

'What does it say? Did she resign? Wouldn't she give some notice?'

Rukia's eyes are fixed on the screen in front of her. She raises her eyebrows a little – not enough for me to be sure I'm not imagining it. Maybe her face hasn't moved at all. 'I'm sorry, I can't share the contents of the email. But Nadine won't be in today, I'm afraid. Or . . .'

'Or ever?' I suggest.

'Right.' Rukia nods. 'Sorry. Is it anything I can help you with?'

I say nothing, remembering Nadine's words: *I can't talk to you. If you're under his spell, you'll tell him anything I say. Tomorrow morning I'll find myself out of a job.*

Tom and I were together until ten last night.

56

Would he have had time to get Nadine fired between then and this morning? I didn't tell him what she said about him, but did I say enough to make him see her as a threat?

'Can I ask you something?' I say to Rukia. 'If Nadine's gone, there's no reason why you shouldn't tell me: did you like her?'

'Like her?'

'Yes. Nadine. Did you trust her? Were the two of you friends?'

'Can't say I knew her that well. We got on okay, yeah. I trusted her as a colleague. I didn't confide in her or anything, but . . . I certainly had no reason not to trust her.'

I ought to stop now. And leave.

'What about Tom Rigbey? Do you like and trust him?'

'Um . . .' Rukia laughs. 'He's our CSO. It's not for the likes of me to have opinions about him.'

'Don't be silly. There's no class system for opinions. Please be honest with me. I really need to know. Is Tom an okay guy, or is there something shady about him?'

'Shady?' Now she's giggling. 'Tom Rigbey, shady? No, not at all. He can be a bit of a buffoon, but he's very sweet.'

'A buffoon?'

'Yeah – certainly compared to most of the

stuffed suits around here. He's also more interesting and fun than them. Tom's a character.
Sometimes he walks along the corridor singing.
He often forgets to take off his bicycle clips.
Once he went into an important meeting with
a smear of bike oil on his cheek. But everyone
here likes him.' Rukia leans towards me and
lowers her voice. 'Don't get me wrong: it helps
that he's oh-my-God gorgeous and a science
genius.'

I breathe out slowly. It's a relief to hear this.
'Do you know why Nadine didn't like him?' I
ask.

'I didn't know she didn't.' Rukia looks
surprised. 'She never said anything to me.'

No, because she didn't need to. Rukia wasn't
in danger, as Nadine saw it.

'Please just tell me one thing: was Nadine
fired?'

Rukia pauses, then nods. 'I don't know what
for. Email doesn't say.'

What could Nadine know about Tom that
Rukia doesn't?

I don't believe he's dangerous. I don't. Even
though Nadine was afraid she'd be fired and
now she has been. It's just . . . if she wanted
to put me off Tom because she was jealous,
wouldn't she have said something less weird

58

like: 'He'll use you for sex and then drop you'
– something like that? Her choice of words
makes it so much harder for me to ignore
what she said. *Avoid him like the plague because
that's what he is . . . Give him nothing, tell him
nothing . . .*

That goes beyond normal bitchiness, surely.

Did Nadine give something to Tom Rigbey
and suffer as a result? Did she tell him a secret
and regret it?

My phone buzzes in my pocket twice. That
means a text or email, not a phone call. It's
not Lorna, then. Lorna would ring. I'm not
taking her calls today, I've decided. She's too
much of a mood-wrecker.

I thank Rukia and leave. Outside on Hills
Road, I pull out my phone. My heartbeat starts
to gallop when I see it's a message from Tom.
'Selfie outside New Bond Street jeweller's shop',
it says. He's signed it 'T xx'. The attached photo
is of Tom standing in front of a window display
of diamond rings, smiling his heart-stopping
smile.

Oh, God. He's going to propose to me
tonight. What else can this mean? What
should I do?

A sneering voice in my head – Lorna's? Nadine
Caspian's? – says *You can't say you haven't been*

warned. Run, Chloe, run. Remember, you have to think of Freya's well-being too.

I'm going to have to ring Lorna, even though the thought of a grilling from her makes my throat close up. I can't think what else to do.

9

'This is such a gripping case study,' Lorna says after a long silence. We're having lunch at The Green Man in Trumpington. Well, she is. I'm staring at a tuna steak I have no desire to eat. 'Can I say what I find most striking? You want to hear my opinion?'

I nod, though 'want' is not quite the right word.

'Tom Rigbey is not keen on you in the normal sense of the word. He's not smitten in a good way. Wanting to see you night after night, talking about diamond rings within milliseconds of meeting you – that's not normal. Wait!' Lorna holds up a hand to stop me saying anything. 'You can argue later. For now, just listen. Tom Rigbey is a stalker – a creepy man who latches on to strangers. Most women would run a mile from anyone who came on so scarily strong so quickly, but you didn't. Until I said "stalker", you didn't think of him as one, did you?'

'No.' I blink away tears. Maybe I'm naïve.

Maybe falling for a charming, handsome, thoughtful science genius who is nicer to me than anyone else I've ever met is the height of stupidity. I'd be a better person, no doubt, if I accused strangers of being creepy, like Lorna does. 'Tom isn't a stalker,' I say.

'Yes, he totally is. You don't see it for a very simple reason: you're one too.' Lorna smiles proudly. 'Like I said: the two of you make for a compelling case study. I'm almost tempted to contact a psychology professor. Most victims of stalkers hate it and see the stalking for what it is. But imagine if a stalker happens to prey on someone who's never had enough love or attention – prey, maybe, on someone whose mother has always been a doormat for one husband after another, and who was always expected to take second place and fit in. This woman with the man-pleasing mother doesn't have such a great romantic past, by the way.'

'I'd never have guessed,' I murmur.

'In her twenties, she follows her mother's bad example and falls for the wrong guy: a chancer who's terrified of commitment, and before she knows what's hit her, he's gone, leaving her with a baby and a broken heart.'

'Lorna?'

'What?'

'I'm not going to be any less offended because you're saying "she" instead of "you". You don't need to talk about me in the third person.'

'Offended? Don't be offended.'

'Oh, okay then.'

'And don't be sarcastic either. You came to me because you wanted to understand what's going on here, and you couldn't. I've worked it out. I'm helping you. Tom Rigbey, quite by chance, chose as his latest stalking victim someone so emotionally needy, she can't recognise stalking as stalking. You!'

Lorna stares at me in clear delight, as if I'm a rabbit she's just pulled out of a hat. 'Wait! I know what you're going to say: you don't see yourself as emotionally needy because you're not clingy and pushy in the way that most needy people are. On the contrary; you never ask for anything.'

Lorna takes a break from attacking my character to sip her ginger beer shandy. She slurps in her eagerness to get going again, and spills a bit out of the side of her mouth.

'I've never thought about this before, but I reckon there are two types of needy,' she goes on, wiping her chin. 'Active and passive. Active is . . . Glenn Close's character in *Fatal Attraction*. She's the perfect example. Passive – or maybe secret is a better word – is you. No one would know you were needy, least of all you, because you ask for nothing and expect nothing. You go through life accepting that you'll never be special, never be anyone's favourite. Why should you be, right? Ordinary little old you? You neither hope nor expect to get your needs met, so, like a dutiful parent, you feed all your energy into caring for Freya.

'But then, boom! Out of the blue, Tom Rigbey comes along like a bolt of lightning . . . He's hugely needy too, by the way, though he uses his wit and charm to hide the emptiness inside him. His good looks too – no one suspects how desperate he is because, come on, who wouldn't be really confident if they looked like that?'

Desperate. The word lodges at the centre of my mind, in the bulls-eye spot.

Lorna's right. Who would think about marriage so early in a relationship unless they were desperate? Not even a relationship, come to think of it. Not even a friend yet: an acquaintance. Why would a brilliant, handsome man like Tom Rigbey waste his time with me, unless . . .

Unless he's so insecure that he'd fear rejection if he targeted a woman in the same league as him.

'Tom Rigbey, your knight-in-shining-armour,'

Lorna warms to her theme. 'He saves the day, gets Freya's music to the *Joseph* auditions in time to avoid disaster, heaps flattery on both you and her, mentions diamonds and marriage terrifyingly quickly. At this point, any regular woman would think, "Yikes, a stalker!", but not you – because, unknown to you, you've secretly always craved that kind of attention. To you he doesn't seem single-minded and obsessive – he seems pleasingly attentive! Gratifyingly keen! I notice you're not denying it.'

That's because I've lost the power of speech.

'You respond to his stalking by *stalking him back*.' Lorna couldn't be more delighted by her own cleverness. 'You make him a tie-pin with musical notes inside it from a song that's supposed to have some meaning for the two of you – *way* over the top, as thank-you gifts go. You stay up half the night Googling him—'

'As did you,' I point out.

'Only because I knew you were, and I guessed you'd make a hash of it. Then you take the present to his office when you could easily have posted it. Why didn't you? You were hoping to bump into him, that's why. And then you let him take you out for dinner, and agree to another dinner the next night, despite being warned about him . . .'

'By a stranger!' I snap. 'Would you take the word of a stranger – one who refused to explain what she meant – and avoid someone you liked, who had only ever been nice to you?'

Lorna pulls her face out of her pint glass and sighs. 'Not nice, Chloe. Stalkerish. Please see sense. Look, think of it like this: imagine you meet a man who has this weird habit of constantly edging forward with his feet when he speaks to you. You'd find it annoying, wouldn't you? You're trying to talk to him but you can't concentrate because all the time he's shuffling closer and closer. Soon his face will be touching yours – eww! *Unless* . . . can you guess where I'm going with this?'

Outer Mongolia? I should be so lucky.

'Unless *you* have the equally weird habit of constantly edging *backwards* whenever you have a chat, at exactly the same rate that he edges forward. Then you wouldn't notice. You'd both be weirdos, but your weirdnesses would be hidden when you were together. They'd cancel each other out. See what I mean?'

'Unfortunately, yes.'

Saying that I see doesn't stop Lorna from wanting to tell me again. 'Both you and Tom Rigbey are keen stalkers and grateful to be stalked at the same time. Hence you're both able to maintain the illusion that you're just two normal people who are attracted to one another. Mystery solved!'

'Not the Nadine mystery,' I say.

'Yes, Chloe! Ugh, get real. When Nadine described him as a plague and a danger, that must have been what she meant. Maybe he came on strong to her the way he is with you. She found it frightening and told him to sod off. He then did something horrid to her as payback for the rejection – God knows what – and that's what she was hinting at. Chloe, Nadine was sacked *hours* after you mentioned her name to Tom, because you told him you thought she might be jealous. If that doesn't convince you, nothing will. He clearly panicked about what she might say to you if you met her again, and decided to get shot of her, fast.'

'You say "clearly", but it's not clear. It's speculation.'

'No, it's fact. Tom Rigbey is unhealthily obsessed with you. You don't see it because you're equally unhealthily obsessed with him. Something disastrous is almost definitely going to happen here! Men like that, who treat you like a goddess and call you "Ma'am" . . . they're the ones who end up caving in your skull with a metal pipe when you burn their dinner and suddenly they see you're not perfect. Take my advice and heed Nadine's warning.'

'No.'

'Chloe, you don't know what he did to her! What would someone have to do to you to make you call them a plague in human form? Set fire to your house? Plant a bomb in your car?'

Something about these two suggestions makes my brain jolt. It's the strangest feeling: my mind turns full-circle and, at the end of it, everything looks different.

It's obvious what I need to do. Lorna is saying something, but I don't hear her properly. I'm thinking.

'Chloe!' Lorna snaps her fingers in front of my face. 'Did you hear what I just said?'

'Yes.' Sort of. It was something about her knowing someone who could probably help me. 'I don't need help.'

Lorna sprays shandy across the table in her effort not to laugh. 'You forgot to add "with my insanity". Tough,' she says. 'You're getting help whether you want it or not. They're only in Cambridge for a couple more days – it's too good a chance to miss. And . . .' She glances at her watch. 'At the risk of pissing you off still further, I've made the arrangement already.

We'd better get a move on – we're meeting them in twenty minutes.'

'Who?' I ask.

Lorna rolls her eyes. 'I knew you weren't listening,' she says.

10

'They' turn out to be Lorna's old school friend Charlotte and her husband Simon. We've met them in The Eagle. Both are police officers. He's some kind of hotshot murder detective. She's more in the social-work sphere of policing: community crime forums, suicide prevention, that kind of thing.

I don't want to be here, but I can't deny I'm finding them interesting so far. I'm enjoying wondering about them. She, Charlotte, seems to flinch every time Lorna speaks, which makes me warm to her.

Her husband has hardly said a word, and keeps beaming the fiercest of evil stares at anyone nearby who laughs or clinks their glass too loudly. But I'm pleased with him because, when we arrived, he asked if we could move to a quieter part of the pub. Thanks to him, we're sitting in the room I always want to sit in and am never normally allowed to by Lorna because it doesn't have enough history – the one to the right of the front door.

Why is Simon so uptight about normal pub noise? It's odd. Also strange is their reason for being in Cambridge. Apparently Charlotte's sister is staying at the Varsity Hotel for a week with her boyfriend. That's what they said, with no more detail except 'We're here to spy on them'. Perhaps that was a joke and the four are all on holiday together, but that wasn't my impression. Charlotte made it sound more as if she and Simon were on some kind of stake-out.

I feel guilty for taking up their time, and weak for allowing Lorna to bring me here and subject me to this. I close my eyes and try to magic myself out of the room while she tells the story so far in her own special way.

Once she's finished, Charlotte says, 'Chloe? You haven't said anything. Do you disagree with Lorna?'

I don't know what to say. I'm sure of my answer, but I feel no need to share my opinion. It would be rude to say nothing, though, and I don't want to be rude to anyone who prefers me to Lorna, as Charlotte seems to.

'There's no proof of anything,' I say. 'Maybe

Tom's dangerous, but maybe Nadine Caspian got it wrong. Or was just plain lying for some reason. I don't know. I can't judge without evidence.'

Lorna can't let that go. 'There's no absolute proof, but there's plenty of indirect evidence,' she says. 'More than enough for a guilty verdict, in my view.' So now she's making a court case out of it: I'm the defence to her prosecution. I pity the judges. I bet they wish they'd never agreed to meet us.

'Chloe's right that what Nadine says is hearsay only,' says Charlotte.

Thank you.

'Nadine got fired,' Simon says. 'She was worried she'd get fired if she spoke up, and she did. I agree with Lorna that her use of extreme language – the plague stuff – makes a real threat more likely. Not only because of the language itself, but because of what went before it.'

'What do you mean?' I ask him.

'The conversation you and Nadine had before you mentioned Tom Rigbey's name, assuming Lorna retold it correctly. There were no unusual turns of phrase. The opposite, in fact. She spoke in clichés: "have a nosey", "the man in your life", "a prezzie for me, and it's not even my birthday". Then when you mentioned Rigbey, her speech became more distinctive: "give him nothing, tell him nothing, trust him not at all". That's almost poetic, and really sticks in the mind. "A plague in human form" – also strong and attention-grabbing. It's not evidence of anything, but if I had to guess, I'd say a sudden burst of fear or anger, sparked off by hearing Rigbey's name when she didn't expect to, caused her to switch from clichés to vivid expression.'

I nod and try to look as if I welcome this insight.

'On the other hand . . .' Simon scratches his badly shaved chin. 'I don't know. From what you've told us, Rigbey's handsome, confident, successful. Probably more dazzling and brilliant than his colleagues. Put someone like that in a workplace and you'll see an outbreak of Tall Poppy Syndrome – people will set out to mow him down.'

'Not the admin staff, surely?' Charlotte says. 'Is it likely that Nadine the receptionist would be jealous of the CSO? I reckon she's more likely to envy a better-paid receptionist.'

'Woman scorned,' Simon mutters. 'That's the simplest answer, if she's lying about Rigbey. Which means it's unlikely to be that.'

'It's unlikely to be the simplest answer?' I say, wondering if I've misheard.

Simon nods. 'Nothing is simple, ever. The true explanation for anything you don't understand is likely to be so complex, you'll never fully grasp it.'

'How comforting,' says Lorna dryly. 'I disagree. The simplest answer is that Tom Rigbey's dangerous and best avoided. Anyone who can't fully grasp that wants their head looked at! He butted into Chloe's conversation with Freya and demanded that she hand over her car keys. He smarmed up to Freya, calling her "Your Highness", sucking up to her to win Chloe over. Then, after getting Chloe's present, he stakes out Freya's rehearsal, knowing Chloe will be there, and in their next conversation – only the second they've ever had – he mentions marriage and hints at diamond rings. As if that's not enough, he jokingly refers to locking Freya in a cellar.'

'It was a joke,' I say to myself more than anyone else.

'Yeah, one that tells us a lot about him.' Lorna's eyes flare with anger. 'His idea of humour is interesting. It seems to consist of . . . lying, basically. "Where did you get the tie-pin from? Oh, I know: the Folk Song Tie-Pins

Warehouse, just off the M11." We all know no such place exists! I know you'll say that was also only a joke, Chloe, but the fact is Tom Rigbey peppers his small talk with bullshit. So, it's likely he does the same with his . . .' Lorna stops, searching for the right word.

'With his big talk?' I suggest.

'Yes. Every tiny detail – everything! – points in the direction of him being dodgy and unsafe. What about the "If I ever fake my own death" joke? And "Who is this Daniel? I'll have him killed" when you told him your surname? And calling himself "The Talented Mr Rigbey" – that's a nod to The Talented Mr Ripley, a charming and devious fictional *murderer*. A psychopath.'

'That might be stretching a point,' says Simon. 'His name's Tom. Mr Ripley's name: also Tom. The link would occur to most people, I think. If my name were Tom Rigbey, I'm sure I'd make that joke more than once in my life.'

'You wouldn't,' Charlotte tells him. 'I'd have to make it for you, and you'd get cross with me.'

'How about his ringtone being "The Real Slim Shady"?' Lorna asks. 'Shady means dishonest – not to be trusted. That song is a celebration of all things dodgy.'

'It's just a song,' I mutter. 'A catchy one.'

Lorna goes on, 'What about him saying that Chloe had better not choose *Bridesmaids* or *Pretty Woman* as her favourite film? You don't think that's sinister-control-freaky at all, telling her what movies are acceptable? And look at his favourites: *Whatever Happened to Baby Jane?* – about twisted people who aren't what they first appear to be – and *Prisoners*, a film that comes close to condoning torture.'

'My favourite movies are *Jaws* and *An Officer and a Gentleman*,' says Charlotte. 'I'm neither a naval officer nor a shark.'

'Every single word out of his mouth is just . . . *off*,' says Lorna wearily. I remind myself that she has never heard any of his words – only what I've relayed back to her. 'How can you not see it, Chloe? What about when he joked about the lyrics of *Joseph* being so terrible? You told me he said, "It's just *awful*," gleefully, as if he enjoyed awful things most of all.'

'But you could do that with anyone's speech!' I snap. 'Twist it, analyse it so closely that—'

'There's no point in any of this,' Simon cuts in. 'We're going back and forth, getting nowhere. Chloe, would you like us to check this guy out, put your mind at rest?'

'Yes, she would,' says Lorna.

'Chloe?' Charlotte asks pointedly. I'm grateful to her for noticing that I'm a person with a mind of my own.

I'm torn. Yes, I want to know, especially if there's something about Tom that he'll never tell me. I want to know every single thing about him, the best and the worst, but can I say that without explaining why? No one would understand.

I have to take the risk. I can't pass up this chance. 'Are you allowed to . . . check people out, when they've committed no crime?' I ask.

'No,' says Charlotte. 'So don't tell anyone we did, okay?'

'It depends,' says Simon, as if the question hasn't just been answered. 'If there's possible danger involved, it's a different story.'

'What we're allowed to do and what's the right thing to do aren't always the same thing,' Charlotte tells me.

'My hunch is that if we look, we'll find something of interest,' says Simon. 'I don't like threats that go unnoticed. They tend to grow and keep growing. Plus, I'm curious. I'd send you to Cambridge Police, but they'll do it by the book, so . . . tell me everything you know about Tom Rigbey and I'll get on it. In the meantime, stay away from him.'

I can't do that – I'm having dinner with Tom

tonight – but I'm happy to share everything I know about him with Simon. It's not much.

'He grew up in Manchester,' I say. 'His parents now live in Florida – they moved there five years ago. He has a brother who's a dentist in Fallowfield in Manchester – Julian – and a friend called Keiran who's got a very expensive BMW sports car – a hundred grand, Tom said. Some people broke into it recently and left it full of burger wrappers and cider bottles. He's had one serious relationship with a woman called Maddy. They were together four years, but then she moved to Australia for work.'

'Girlfriend escapes down under, parents flee to Florida,' Lorna mutters. 'Sounds to me like everyone can't wait to get away from The Talented Mr Rigbey.'

'Anything else, Chloe?' Charlotte asks. 'Literally, anything at all might be useful, however daft it seems.'

'Um . . . he told me his Twitter avatar is a photo of an armadillo he saw next to his parents' pool in Florida. He used to have two English Bull Terriers as pets: Butch and Sundance.'

'Butch and Sundance?' Lorna pounces. 'You never told me that!' She turns to Simon. 'Could this *be* any more obvious? Butch Cassidy and the Sundance Kid – two outlaws!'

'Or, if we want to be fair about this . . .' says Charlotte, who seems to like going against Lorna, and is braver than I am, 'English Bull Terriers are a butch-looking breed of dog. Aren't they the ones with the huge sticking-out faces that look as if they're made of rock? If I had a dog like that, the name Butch might well spring to mind.'

'Sundance,' I say quietly. 'Dancing merrily in the sun – must mean Tom's a happy, *innocent* person who loves dancing.'

Charlotte laughs.

'Leave it with us, Chloe,' says Simon. 'Let's meet around five o'clock tomorrow afternoon.'

11

I stand apart from the other parents in the school playground as we wait for the end-of-day bell to ring, and use my phone to search for Nadine Caspian on the internet.

I can't wait a whole day for more information. I have to do something right now. Every nerve in my body is buzzing with a need to act. I might not be a police detective, but I care more than Simon and Charlotte do. And they aren't the only ones who can check things out.

If I can find Nadine's address, I'm going to pay her a visit. She can't say what she said to me then change her mind and vanish. It's not fair.

Her name is unusual. That should make it easier to find her. There can't be many Nadine Caspians in Cambridge.

First I'll force it out of her: what she knows, what she thinks will make me turn my back on Tom. I want to tell her that nothing will. Nothing ever could.

This is what struck me while Lorna was harassing me earlier, over lunch: I've been sick with fear since Nadine said what she said on the stairs at CamEgo, but I shouldn't have been. I only need to worry if it would make a difference – if there is something, anything, I could learn about Tom that would change the way I feel.

That he blew up a building.

If my love for him were based on him being a virtuous, harmless person, then I would – right now – be at the mercy of Nadine, Simon, Charlotte, Lorna. Any of them, at any time, could present me with a previously unknown fact about him that would ruin everything.

That he strangled an elderly relative.

I realised earlier that the opposite is true.

Nothing could put me off Tom. Whatever he's done, whatever he is, I love him and will always love him. I can't help it. There's no point pretending that any moral or principle could change that. I've never felt this way about anyone before. Since our first meeting, there has been no room in my head for anything but Tom Rigbey. I've been floating on the happiness that his existence and interest in me has brought into my life. If he's smuggled drugs or set fire to houses, I don't care. If every word out of his mouth is a lie, so what?

No one else has ever made me feel as happy and excited as I feel in his presence – not even for ten minutes.

Not at all.

So. I have to not care. It's the only way I can be immune to what Simon and Charlotte might be about to find out and tell me.

If Tom is a plague in human form, and I'm ready to accept all of his sins, then I must be one too. Chloe the plague.

I should do something wrong – really horribly wrong – to prove that we belong together, that we're right for each other. Something Nadine Caspian can find out about and say, 'Ugh, Chloe Daniels is every bit as evil as Tom Rigbey. They deserve each other.'

Maybe I could do something wrong *to* Nadine Caspian. Now there's an idea . . .

The school bell rings, startling me, at the exact moment that I find Nadine on Twitter. There's her horrible face as her avatar, smiling. Like a doll made of flesh-coloured stone. I have a quick look up and down her timeline. Her tweets are mostly inane: clothes, booze, cake-baking. Suddenly, a new tweet appears, moving the others down on my phone's screen. She must have just done it. It's a quote. It says, 'Pour yourself a drink put on some lipstick and pull yourself together – Elizabeth Taylor'. There should be a comma after 'drink'.

I press the 'Reply' icon at the bottom of Nadine's latest tweet, and write, 'Why are you so against Tom Rigbey? What's he ever done to you?' Then I press the 'Tweet' button.

Her reply appears on her timeline a few seconds later. 'He's a sociopath. Leave me alone. Blocking you now.'

A sociopath? The word is like cold medicine, making me swallow hard. What does it even mean?

I'll look it up later. If Tom Rigbey is a sociopath, then I must become one too. *Oh, God.* I hold my breath and clench my fists, nearly knocked off balance by sudden weakness. I'm not sure I can do this. *Please let this whole thing be one big mistake.*

'Mum!' Freya calls out, running towards me. 'I won the Star of the Week award!'

'That's wonderful, darling. Well done.' I say all this without taking in what she's told me. I'm too lost in my own thoughts.

If I find out the truth about Tom and say nothing, he'll think I don't know.

The possibility that I know and don't mind because I love him no matter what will not occur to him.

12

'Do you hate it? Tell me if you hate it, and I'll
. . . scoot over and propose to that woman over
there instead. No, I'm kidding. Is it okay?'

I stare tearfully at the large pear-shaped
diamond in its open, cushioned box. 'It's beautiful,' I manage to say. 'Stunning.' Any minute
now, the La Mimosa staff will spot the ring and
this will no longer be a private conversation.

I won't be able to say no, surrounded by
Italian waiters.

I don't want to say no. There's a big, loud
'YES' in my head.

Tom looks delighted. 'Try it on, see if it fits.
If it doesn't, I can get it altered. No, wait! Don't
try it on.'

'Why not?'

'I think you need to accept first – officially.
You need to say you want to marry me. If you
do. If you don't, that's fine. I'll just wade into
the River Cam with my pockets full of heavy
stones. That's why I picked this restaurant – the

river's right outside, full of the bodies of rejected suitors.' He grins. He knows I'm going to say yes.

Am I, though? If not, what's stopping me? Not his over-the-top, weird sense of humour. I like that about him. Other people's chatter has started to seem duller since I met Tom. Every sentence he utters is full of surprises. Listening to him, talking to him, is like unwrapping presents all the time.

What's stopping me accepting Tom's proposal is that I'm not being honest with him. If he knew the truth, he might decide he doesn't love me that much after all. How would he feel if I told him that, earlier today, I asked two police officers to look into his background for me? I could explain that I'd only done it in the hope of finding him to be totally innocent, but would that make it better?

Tom's love for me might not be as strong, as unconditional, as mine for him. I can't take the risk. It's not only that I'm certain he'd be furious if he knew I'd asked two strangers to spy on him. There's something else too. What if he needs to pretend that the mistakes of the past never happened so as to survive in the present? What if part of my appeal for him is that I don't know about the terrible things he did, assuming they're real?

'Chloe? You look worried. Is everything okay?' Tom puts his head in his hands. 'I'm such an idiot,' he says. 'You're an *idiot*, Rigbey! Proposing out of the blue to a woman who barely knows you—'

'No, it's not that,' I try to say, but he talks over me.

'Look, Chloe, I know it's too soon to be thrusting diamond rings in your face. I've just dived straight in, like a reckless kid – I knew it was a risky tactic, but the thing is . . . I spent four years with Maddy, living with her, never sure of whether to propose or not because I just didn't know. I felt as if I ought to want to marry her – sometimes I was almost sure I did – but it also seemed possible that, in fact, I didn't. That living together was enough.

'It wasn't enough for her, though, and when she left for Australia, although I missed her, I wasn't a wreck. I wasn't desperate. I could imagine a life without her. I assumed I was the sort of person who would never feel the urge to marry anybody – which I thought would be fine, because my work's so all-consuming. I thought work was my passion in life.' He stops. Frowns.

'And?' I prompt him.

'And then I saw you on Bridge Street and . . .

well, actually it wasn't only love at first *sight*.
I heard your voice, too. Her Highness might be
the singer of the family, but . . . you have a
lovely voice, Chloe. Even when you're yelling
like a Wall Street trader whose shares have all
just . . . deflated, or whatever shares do. I fell
in love with you, and I thought to myself,
"That's the woman I'm going to marry. That
shouty one over there."'

'Tom – stop.'

'Ah. Okay. Oh dear.' He looks crushed.

'I want to say yes, I really do—'

'You do?' He perks up. 'Excellent! Then say
it.'

'Tom, there are . . . things about me that you
don't know. Things you might not like if you
knew.'

'Such as?'

I hear Nadine Caspian's voice in my head:
Tell him nothing, trust him not at all.

'I wish I could tell you, but I can't,' I say
tearfully.

'Chloe, there are things you don't know
about me too. When I was in my early twenties, I pretended I was allergic to fish. Not just
mildly. I led all my colleagues to believe – well,
I *told* them – that if I swallowed so much as a
drop of fish oil, I'd very likely die.'

I laugh, while trying not to cry. I am an emotional rainbow. 'Er . . . why?'

'Long story. The simple answer is youthful folly. Basically, I went out drinking one night with friends when I should have been getting an early night before an important work away-day. Next morning I was unable to do anything except puke into a bucket. I was too sick to stagger to the bathroom. If I'd told my boss the truth, he'd have thought, rightly, that he ought to promote someone else – someone less wild and more responsible. I thought of giving a lame excuse like food poisoning, but no one would have believed it, so in a moment of panic I trotted out a story that no one would think to doubt because it was so . . . extreme. And tragic, too. Poor me: ever-present risk of ghastly early death from eating haddock, what a great loss, etcetera.'

'But . . . in the story, how did you explain why you'd eaten fish if you were so allergic?' If I'd been Tom's girlfriend in those days, I could have helped him to avoid basic continuity errors.

'A very good question.' Tom chuckles. 'As I recall, my story involved a curry house kitchen allowing a sliver of cod to fall into my Kofta Madras. Everyone at work was very concerned, just as I'd cunningly planned. I got the promotion, and was stuck with a fake allergy. Keeping up the pretence was so tiring, I left within a year and started a new life at a different firm, where I soon showed myself to be a keen fish eater.'

'I've never seen you eat fish,' I tell him, looking at the chicken liver pâté on his plate. 'You've always ordered meat when I've had meals with you. Not even a prawn cocktail starter.'

'Wait – you're accusing me of lying about *not* having a fish allergy?' Tom teases me.

'Do you think anyone can ever really trust anyone?' I ask him.

'Yes. I trust you,' he says. 'Now, since you've heard mine, please spill all your guilty secrets. I promise you: you won't put me off.'

Yes, because he's a stalker. Lorna's voice this time.

I wish they'd shut up, all these more-sensible-people-than-me who have somehow managed to invade my mind. I need to be able to hear my own thoughts, form my own opinions.

'Or, if you'd prefer, you can remain a mystery,' Tom suggests. 'I like a good mystery. If you want to keep quiet about your shady past as a drug kingpin, that's fine by me. What is a kingpin, by the way? I'm not sure I've ever known, but I think I might like to be one.'

I love him. And I've never heard the word 'shady' said in such a wholesome way.

'Yes,' I say.

'Yes what? Oh!' Tom's eyes widen. 'You mean . . . *yes*, yes?'

'Yes. *Yes*, yes.'

'You'll marry me?'

'Haven't you had enough yeses yet?' I take the diamond ring from the box and slide it onto my finger. 'It's a bit loose. Sorry.'

'Damn. I'd better order you another pizza with extra cheese – fatten you up.' Suddenly Tom looks worried. 'Do you want to check with Freya before saying *yes*, yes?'

'No. If she complains, I'll put her up for adoption.' I laugh. Tom doesn't.

Sorry. Just a little sociopath joke there.

I think of *West Side Story*, the musical my sixth-form college put on when I was seventeen. Tom is right: I do have a nice voice. Long before Freya was born, I was the singer of the family. As Maria in *West Side Story,* I sang, 'I love him. I'm his. And everything he is, I am too.' I sing those words again now, in my head.

'I think it should be fine?' Tom says as if he's

asking a question. 'Freya likes me, doesn't she? Damn, maybe the forgotten-music rescue dash wasn't enough. I might have to buy a God costume, appear in her room in the middle of the night and say in a deep booming voice that I decree Tom Rigbey must marry her mother and nothing must stand in his way.'

'Oh, I thought you were already wearing your God costume,' I say dryly. 'I assumed you had it on long-term loan from the costume shop.'

For the first time since we met, Tom laughs at my joke as much as I laugh at all of his.

13

The next day, Lorna and I meet Simon and Charlotte again – not at The Eagle this time, but, oddly, at the market's waffle stall in the square. Simon's choice because, Lorna says, he didn't like The Eagle yesterday. It seems neither Charlotte nor Lorna could come up with another indoor venue that he liked.

What the hell's wrong with him? Why didn't he like The Eagle? How can an open-to-the-weather market stall be the best option? It's cold, windy, raining, and the four of us are shivering in plastic chairs around a wobbly table. Our heads are shielded from the rain by a canvas cover, but we're still getting damp because it's blowing in sideways. Simon didn't even order a waffle – just a cup of tea. The man who handed it to him, who is now making waffles for the rest of us, keeps shooting puzzled looks at us. I can tell he's thinking, 'Why on earth do they want to sit here on a day like today?'

One good thing about being freezing cold is

that I can keep my scarf wrapped tightly around my neck and hide the gold chain I don't normally wear. My engagement ring is dangling from the end of it, since it's too loose to wear on my finger, and Lorna would spot it straight away, given half a chance.

Everyone assumed I would cancel my dinner with Tom last night. No one has asked me if I did.

Simon's holding a notebook – the kind only a man would choose, with nothing fancy about it. He's not reading from it yet, but he stares at it as he speaks, as if his words are written down there. 'All right, there's a lot of detail and none of it remarkable, so you'll need to pay attention. I'll repeat it if I have to, but I'd rather not have to.'

I'd rather not be accused in advance of failing to listen properly when I've done nothing wrong. But I don't say so, because I'm more polite than Simon.

'Big picture first, then details,' he says in the same slightly disapproving tone. 'Everything Tom Rigbey told you about himself and his life appears to be true. He's got no criminal record. On paper he's a blameless citizen.'

I'm basking in the warmth of the relief that's flooding my system when Simon adds,

'That's why I said listen carefully. You'll also need to *think* carefully. The answer isn't obvious, but it's here, contained in what you already know and what I'm about to tell you. Once you see it, you can't miss it . . . but you might have to look hard in order to see it.'

Charlotte says, 'I have to say, Chloe, that I haven't a clue what Simon's talking about, and I've heard the whole thing twice already today, so you're not the only one in the dark.'

I don't understand. Isn't she his wife? Why didn't she ask him to explain it to her before they got here? That's what I would have done.

'Tom Rigbey was born in Manchester, in 1981. He has one brother – Julian, the Fallowfield dentist – and a sister, Rebecca. Did he mention her to you?'

'Yes, but not by name. He said they weren't close.'

'They aren't,' Simon agrees. 'She lives in London and works for the CBI.'

'Which is what?' I ask.

'The Confederation of British Industry.'

'Oh.' I'm none the wiser. Okay. Tom's sister works . . . somewhere businessy. That'll do. 'He told me she lived in London.'

'Right. Parents – Fort Lauderdale, Florida, for the last five years, as he said. They have a shared swimming pool at their apartment building, as Tom said, and I've no reason to believe that the armadillo in his Twitter avatar isn't one he photographed beside that pool.'

'Is the armadillo relevant to anything?' Lorna asks crossly.

'Anything might be relevant,' says Charlotte. 'We don't know yet.'

'No,' Simon says flatly. 'The armadillo's got fuck all to do with it. Forget him.'

'Right.' Charlotte mutters. She looks a bit annoyed. We sit in silence for a while. I suspect I'm not the only one disobediently remembering the armadillo.

'Tom's friend Keiran with the expensive BMW – that's also true,' Simon goes on. 'Keiran Connaughton. He and Tom were in the same year at Manchester Grammar School and have stayed friends since. Bear in mind, one sign that someone's a dangerous sociopath is if they have no one in their life who dates back very far – no one able to reveal that they've changed their various stories over the years. But . . . not the case here.'

There's that word again: sociopath.

And if it's not the case that Tom has no long-standing friends, if he's not a sociopath, then what bad and dangerous kind of person is he? What's the problem? Simon's tone and manner suggest there is one and that it's serious. But I can't work out what I'm meant to be listening for.

'The burger-wrappers-and-empty-cider-bottles-in-Keiran's-expensive-sports-car story? True,' he says. 'I've seen no evidence that Tom is dishonest. Butch and Sundance, the Bull Terriers? True.'

'You contacted Keiran?' I say, surprised.

'Charlie spoke to him.'

'Charlie?'

'Me,' says Charlotte. 'Everyone calls me Charlie except Lorna, who refuses to.'

'It's horribly unisex,' Lorna explains.

'Can we not get sidetracked?' says Simon. 'Maddy, the ex-girlfriend, is in Australia where she's supposed to be. She had only good things to say about Tom. So, let's move on to his education and work history. After Manchester Grammar School for boys, he was a student and then a graduate student at King's College, here in Cambridge. He got the best results in his year when he graduated, and he's worked for three companies since. He started his career at Sagentia, just outside Cambridge. Got promoted through the ranks very quickly there. Then he went to Intel, who we've all heard of, and worked there for a few years, in America.'

I've heard of Intel, but I can't say I'm sure what it is. A computer company? Tom has never told me he lived and worked in America. My stomach tenses. Is it coming now, the shocking news?

'He got promoted once at Intel, stayed there for four years, then made another move: back to England, to CamEgo. He's been promoted twice since he got there, and now holds the top job that someone in his field can: CSO.'

Finally, Simon looks up, in time to see three waffles with toffee sauce and maple syrup heading towards our table. 'That's it,' he says. 'That's everything I found out. All of you now know as much as I do.'

14

The sugar rush from my waffle – which is probably delicious, but I barely taste it – ought to make my brain move faster, but it's not working. Neither is the caffeine from my second cup of tea. 'I don't get it,' I tell Simon. 'I listened as carefully as I've ever listened to anything – I don't need you to repeat a single word – but I didn't hear anything worrying or suspicious.'

'Me neither,' says Charlie.

Simon jerks his head at Lorna. 'What about you?'

She'll never admit she spotted nothing. Never. After a few seconds, she says, 'Tom's three jobs – did he move by choice from company to company, or was he sacked? You say he "went" from Sagentia to Intel, then "made another move" to CamEgo . . .'

Simon lurches forward, nearly knocking over our flimsy plastic table. 'That's the question I

98

was hoping to hear.' He looks happy, or what I assume is happy for him. Not grumpy, anyway.

'I think it's a daft question,' I say. 'Sorry, Lorna, but . . . Intel, CamEgo – these are serious companies. He wouldn't have got a job at either without amazing references from his previous companies, would he? And he wouldn't have got those if he'd been fired.'

'Are you sure?' Simon asks me.

My breath catches in my throat. 'No, but—'

'Don't guess. Focus on what we know. Facts. Proven ones. When were you planning to tell me you tweeted Nadine Caspian yesterday?'

'You did *what*?' says Lorna.

'Do you want me to find out the truth for you or not?' Simon glares at me. 'If you do, tell me everything.'

'Simon!' Charlie hits his arm with her plastic fork, leaving a smear of toffee sauce on his coat sleeve. 'Chloe isn't a criminal. She doesn't have to tell you a single thing more than she wants to.'

'I only didn't mention it because I thought it was neither here nor there,' I say, feeling my face heat up.

'Yeah, well, luckily I found it, and it points the same way as everything else. Your tweet to

99

Nadine: "What have you got against Tom Rigbey?" or words to that effect. Hers to you: "He's a sociopath. Leave me alone. You're blocked." You didn't find that interesting?'

'No.' I blink away tears. 'I found it nasty and a slur and . . .'

'A slur?' Simon leaps on the word. 'Because she didn't back it up with facts?'

'No, she didn't.'

'She gave you only one word to go on: sociopath. Still, it's a big one, as words go. Has Tom said anything to you about being fired? Sorry, I'll reword that: has he ever mentioned why he left either Sagentia or Intel?'

'No! I've hardly had a chance to speak to him about anything. We've only just met.'

And yet you're wearing a diamond ring – a ring that means you intend to marry him – on a chain around your neck.

'Why would they promote him and promote him . . . and then fire him?' I ask.

'To be clear,' says Simon. 'Tom has never said anything to you about being fired from . . . anywhere?'

'No! Nothing.'

I don't know why I do what I do next. Perhaps I'm keen to have the worst over with. I remove my scarf, hook my finger around the gold chain and pull it out so that the ring is visible. 'You might as well know. I had dinner with him last night. We're engaged.'

'Jesus fucking Christ on a fucking cracker!' Lorna yells.

'Aren't you training to be some kind of vicar?' Charlie asks her.

'Good,' says Simon.

'*Good*?' I repeat, baffled.

'Yeah. It was the next thing I was going to urge you to do: stop avoiding him, and behave towards him exactly as you would if you weren't suspicious of him. I was going to say: if he proposes, which you seemed to think he might, say yes. Might seem like odd advice, but you'll understand in due course.' Simon shrugs. 'You've already seen him and agreed to marry him, though, so. No need for me to steer things that way.'

'Urgh!' Charlie groans. 'Simon – sorry about this, Chloe – just *tell* her, and tell us all while you're at it. Why can't we find out right now instead of in due course?'

'Yes, especially if you're planning to use Chloe as some kind of bait,' Lorna agrees. 'She needs to know what level of risk she's dealing with. How dangerous is Tom Rigbey?'

'Simon.' Charlie waves her hand in front of

his face. He appears to have drifted into a kind of trance. 'If you've found out that Tom was sacked from one or both of his previous jobs, tell us. Why was he fired?'

Simon fixes his eyes on me: an intense stare. 'I assume you looked up the meaning of sociopathy, after reading Nadine's tweet?'

I nod.

'So you know that a key trait of sociopaths is that they can't hold down a job or stay in one place for very long?'

'Tom's been at CamEgo for long enough to be promoted several times,' I say. 'Talented people often change jobs – other companies make them great offers to get them to move.'

'Sociopaths with forged references change jobs a lot too,' says Simon. 'Whoever checks that references are from the person they're meant to be from?'

'Simon, stop tormenting her,' murmurs Charlie. 'Whatever you've found out, whatever you know . . . seriously. Out with it.'

'Not found out,' he says. 'Worked out. You really can't see it? None of you?'

'No, we can't,' Lorna speaks for all of us. 'I did pretty well guessing Tom had been fired, but there's a limit to how much we can guess.'

'Apparently there is,' says Simon bitterly. This

is beyond belief. He's angry with us for not being mind-readers.

'So Tom got fired. So what?' I say. 'I don't care. Who hasn't been fired at some point or another?' I haven't, but that's beside the point. I can pretend I have if it comes to it. If that's what I have to do to stand by Tom, I'll do it. 'Did he get fired for pretending to have a food allergy?'

'What in the ever-loving name of fuck?' Lorna whirls round to face me. 'Where did that come from?'

'No. What makes you say that?' Simon asks me.

'Nothing. Forget it.'

'Come on.' Suddenly, Simon stands up. 'No, not all of you. Just Chloe. We're going to see Nadine Caspian. You need to hear her story. Until you do, you won't understand. It's not going to be easy for her to tell it, or for you to believe it, but it's the only way.'

15

Half an hour later, Simon and I are outside
Nadine Caspian's house: a beige three-storey
new-build – part of a large square of similar
houses.

'Ready?' says Simon.

I nod. Yes, I'm ready, but for what?

He rings the bell, then stands and stares at
it as if expecting it to reply to him.

I'm wearing my engagement ring on my
wedding finger because he told me to. I didn't
want to without knowing why, but I did it. I
don't want to have to see or speak to Nadine
Caspian, but here I am: bribed by the promise
that soon I will know everything.

Without warning, tears fill my eyes – tears
that had better be gone by the time Nadine
opens the door, or by the time Simon turns to
look at me, whichever happens first. I blink
frantically. Squeeze my eyes shut.

That's better.

I hate this. Not only the doubts about Tom,

but also I hate that this used to be my thing to wonder about – my problem, mine alone – and I seem to have handed over control to . . . well, to everybody. I'm not in charge of anything, least of all myself. And I want to be. If I were braver, I'd take Freya and go somewhere far away from Lorna, Simon the weird policeman, Nadine Caspian . . . I don't want any of these people in my life, so why are they?

Don't be silly – Lorna's your best friend.

And Tom? Do you want him in your life?

Yes, I do. Whoever he is, whatever he's done, I want him. I love him. I'm also frightened that loving him might be about to get harder. So far, I've been able to defend him because I believe in his innocence, but what if that's about to change? What if he did something shocking and impossible to forgive, something for which no excuse can ever be made, and what if I still don't stop loving him even then?

'Come on,' Simon breathes, pressing the bell again.

'She might be out,' I say, and he looks angry.

My phone buzzes in my pocket. I pull it out and look at the screen. 'It's a text from Tom.'

'Show me,' says Simon.

Of course: my fiancé might be a dangerous sociopath, so from now on I must hand over all private messages to the police.

I pass my phone to Simon. Tom has sent a photo of himself sitting at a table in what might be the CamEgo staff canteen. There is a salmon fillet and some rice on a plate in front of him. His message says, 'See? No fish allergy! T xx'

'Text back as if nothing's wrong,' Simon orders. I flinch at what this must mean. 'It's some kind of joke, so be jokey in your reply. Send kisses back – whatever you'd normally do. You're his trusting fiancée as far as he knows, so act like it.'

Nothing is wrong. Nothing is wrong.

I start to compose a message to Tom: 'Fish on plate, not in mouth – not proof of eating! Pictures or it didn't happen, as my friend Lorna would say. C xx'

'Wait – she's coming.' Simon moves closer to the door. 'I heard something move inside.' He presses the bell a third time. 'Let me see that before you send it.'

Too numb to do anything but obey, I show him my reply.

'Good. That's good.' He smiles as if he hasn't had much practice. His mouth looks like a

Venetian blind that's been hoiked up too far on one side.

A serious crime must be involved, or he wouldn't be here. He wouldn't care enough to give up his time. I feel sick. Unreal.

The door in front of us opens and I'm face-to-face with Nadine again. She's wearing black tracksuit bottoms and a pink cotton hoodie. Her eyes widen. 'How did you . . .?' She gawps at me.

'How did she know where to find you?' Simon completes her sentence for her. 'She didn't. I found you.' He pulls out a small flip-open wallet and holds it in front of Nadine's face. 'DC Simon Waterhouse, Culver Valley Police.'

Nadine laughs. 'A detective? From the back of beyond, but still – why am I getting a visit from a detective? Whatever she's told you—'

'She hasn't been able to tell me anything because you haven't told her anything, but that's going to change. Today. Now. No more dropping hints and running away. The three of us are going to have a proper talk. Can we come in?'

'No! You can piss off, is what you can do.'

Simon grabs my left hand and pulls me forward. 'Look – see this ring? It's an engagement ring. Looks pricey, doesn't it? Biggest diamond I've ever seen on a real person's finger.'

I wonder how many fake people's fingers he's seen. I wonder if I'll be wondering about fakes for the rest of my life: fake fingers, fake fish allergies . . .

'I'm guessing you can work out what it means. Tom Rigbey asked Chloe to marry him last night and she said yes.'

Nadine is staring at my ring as if it's a crushed cockroach.

Simon says, 'Chloe didn't listen to your warning, it seems. If you want her to, you're going to need to tell her more. If you don't, I will.'

Scorn contorts Nadine's face. 'How can you tell her what you don't know?'

'I know enough. Speros, Jackson and Decker . . . And you're going to fill in the rest. Let us in.'

What? Speros, Jackson, Decker? The names mean nothing to me. Nadine looks frightened. She understands. I don't.

She opens the door wider and steps back so that her back is flat against the wall. Simon, still holding my arm, pulls me into the house after him.

There is no chit-chat, no offers of cups of tea or glasses of water. In silence, we walk up the stairs to the first floor lounge. It's tidy, with beige walls, a wooden floor and white furniture – furry white pouffes in front of the chairs instead of foot-stools. The fireplace is the smallest I've ever seen, and looks wrong. This is a modern room with a balcony above the garden. It doesn't need, and shouldn't have, a fireplace.

There's a glass coffee table in the middle of the floor. On it are some magazines and two bottles of nail varnish: one dark green and one silver. There are three framed prints on the walls, matching ones: cats with triangular, glittery faces. I've seen these pictures before on cards in shops. Maybe not these exact ones, but the same kind.

'Go on,' Simon says to Nadine once we're all sitting down. 'Time to give Chloe the facts she deserves. Tell her – tell us both – your story. The truth. Leave nothing out.'

'It's difficult for me to talk about,' she says.

'Yeah, I bet it is.' Simon shows no pity. 'Why don't you start with Speros? That was the first one, wasn't it? Then Jackson and Decker next. Then CamEgo. Where next, Nadine?'

Silence.

Questions are racing round my mind, but I mustn't say anything. Simon asks the questions. He's made that very clear. I'm the listener, passive and tame, about to be rewarded with the truth. *Keep your mouth shut, Chloe.*

'Funny how you were so eager to chat when you warned Chloe to stay away from Tom,' Simon tells Nadine. 'Yet now you can't seem to say anything at all. Why is that?'

'Someone please tell me what's going on, before I go crazy,' I blurt out. 'What's Speros? Who are Jackson and Decker? Are those other companies Tom worked for? Did they get rid of him?'

Simon turns to face me. 'Why do you ask that? Is it because I told you Tom had been fired?'

'Yes. And now you're mentioning names I've never heard of that sound like companies.'

'You're wrong, Chloe. You're too easy to trick. If you think back over what I said at the market stall, you'll realise I never said that Tom had been fired from anywhere. He hasn't. He's never been anything but a perfect employee.'

'What? But you said—'

'I asked you if he'd said anything to you about being fired. I asked if he'd told you why he left either Sagentia or Intel.'

'Yes, and you said Lorna's question was the right one, when she asked if he'd been sacked.'

'It was the right one. I wanted to get you all thinking along those lines: people being fired.'

'You also said sociopaths tend not to be able

110

to hold down jobs for very long, and have to fake references to get new jobs.'

'Yeah, I did. But I never said any of that applied to Tom Rigbey, did I?'

'I don't remember! I don't memorise every word you say, I'm sorry.'

'Take it from me,' says Simon. 'I didn't. Tom Rigbey's never been fired. He isn't a sociopath. Yes, sociopaths often get sacked. Who do you know that's been sacked recently, Chloe? Anyone spring to mind?'

What could he mean?

Only one thing.

Having stopped for a second, the world starts to turn again, in a different direction.

'You,' I breathe, staring at Nadine.

'At last.' Simon sounds relieved. 'Chloe Daniels, meet Nadine Caspian the sociopath.'

16

'I'm not any label that applies to a group of people,' says Nadine. If she's shocked or hurt to be described as a sociopath, she doesn't show it. 'I'm me. An individual.'

'One who's been fired three times now,' says Simon. 'And for the same thing in all three cases. It's an unusual kind of offence, I'll grant you that. As you say: individual. At Speros Engineering, you picked on a man called Martin Kennett – like Tom Rigbey, Kennett was a man way above you in rank. He was A-list – you were more like C. You were friendly and helpful to him to his face, but every so often you'd take someone aside – someone you thought might be about to get close to him, someone who seemed to think well of him – and you'd warn them about him. "Keep away from Martin Kennett – he's bad news, seriously bad," you'd tell them. You probably put it more poetically, I'd imagine, since you described Tom Rigbey as a plague. You don't want to deny any of this?'

'That I warned people about Martin? No.' Nadine smiles. 'I think it's important to warn people, even if it's not what they want to hear. It's for their own good.'

'At Speros your hints were taken seriously at first and some people did keep their distance from Kennett. But you were fired when you shared your poisonous warnings with one person too many. Eventually, someone who trusted their own judgement refused to be swayed, and instead thought, "Hang on a minute. There's no way Martin Kennett's evil or dangerous, and no one should be trying to blacken another person's name at work without hard facts to back up her story."

'I don't know who that person was, Nadine,' Simon goes on. 'The bloke I spoke to at Speros wouldn't tell me her name. Maybe you know it? Anyway, whatever her name was, she went to her boss and made a fuss. Martin Kennett versus Nadine Caspian became an official matter, and guess what? You had nothing to back up your claims and hints, did you? You were shown up for what you are: a spiteful troublemaker who picks on innocent people at random, then warns others about them. That's *all* you do – but it's enough.'

'Don't you think it's important to warn

people when you see dangers they don't see?'
Nadine asks. 'As a policeman, I'm sure you issue
warnings all the time.'

'It's a clever tactic, if you want to destroy
other people and their relationships,' Simon
goes on as if she hasn't spoken.

I've never heard a conversation like this
before. Both of them seem to be trapped in
their own private worlds, speaking but not
hearing. I'm frozen – unable to join in, trying
to listen hard and remember every word.

'Jackson and Decker, exactly the same story,'
says Simon. 'This time it was the Managing
Director you chose as your victim, Iain Jackson.
You took people into corners and told them
not to trust him. You said it in a way that
implied a detailed history, untold suffering . . .
and it was bullshit. Lies. All made up. You had
no reason to think Iain Jackson was any more
dangerous than anyone else at Jackson and
Decker.

'As with Speros, you weren't careful enough
about who you spoke to. You told one person,
in the end, who wasn't content to avoid Jackson
from that moment on, purely on your say-so.
He made an issue of it, demanded proof, and
you had none. He started to suspect you were
the person everyone needed to be warned

about. A short while later, you got fired for the second time. Then it happened again at CamEgo – your third sacking in four years.'

Simon turns to me. 'Chloe, when you heard Nadine had lost her job, you feared Tom had made it happen. You thought you'd told him enough to make him think she was onto him. Not true. There was nothing to be onto. Nadine was on her way to getting the boot anyway. Several people at CamEgo were wise to her antics – people who like and are loyal to Tom. But it was the conversation you had with her at CamEgo's offices that speeded up the process. Your conversation took place on the stairs, didn't it?'

'Yes.' I didn't mention that to Simon – where we were when Nadine said those horrible things. Someone else has told him. He's clearly been thorough in his research.

'You were overheard,' Simon tells Nadine. 'On the other side of a thin wall was another flight of stairs leading up to the next floor. Someone coming down those stairs, another CamEgo employee, heard every nasty lie you told. He heard you describe Tom Rigbey as a plague in human form and, knowing this was as far from the truth as it's possible to get, he went to his line manager. That person happened to have been told only the day before about your efforts to badmouth Tom.'

Nadine has a sneer on her face. 'I've done nothing worse than advise people to be careful, DC . . . I can't remember your surname.'

'Waterhouse. Is that your best defence?'

'It's short and to the point.'

'Yes, in keeping with your preferred method,' Simon agrees. 'Say as little as possible. You don't need to kill, maim or inflict injury to have an effect. That would be too easy. Any fool armed with a weapon can destroy – where's the fun in that? You do nothing but warn. If hopes and lives are shattered as a result, it's so much more pleasing for you because you've barely put yourself out at all. What's strange is that you can't see it's *your* life you're trashing. How many more jobs are you happy to lose? Why don't you stop?'

Nadine leans forward and taps the glass coffee table with her fingernail. 'Name one claim I've made that's untrue. All I did was express my own opinion to Chloe. I'm allowed to have an opinion.'

'It's not your true opinion,' says Simon. 'I think you go out of your way to pick blameless victims. And/or stand-out successes, like Tom Rigbey. That makes it more fun, does it, when you bring them down? Except – have you noticed? – you fail every time.

'Luckily for the world, and unluckily for you, there are plenty of people who hear warnings of the sort you dish out and don't just think, "No smoke without fire" and reject someone they previously liked. Luckily, Chloe chose to ignore you and is now engaged to Tom Rigbey. She could see he was a decent guy, even if she couldn't see at first what a toxic person you are.'

'Toxic?' Nadine laughs. 'Toxic because I warned her, as a friend would? Isn't that what we do when we care about each other? Spot the dangers that might lie in store for our friends and warn them?' Her mouth twists into a smile that looks all wrong: creepy and cold. 'Warn them until they don't trust their own judgement any more, and will take our word for anything? I'm sure you've done it, DC Simon,' Nadine goes on. 'Oh, yes, you have! You're doing it now: warning Chloe not to trust me, when you don't know me from Adam. How's that any different to what I said to Chloe about Tom? You can't know what kind of wonderful friendship Chloe and I might have had if your "toxic" slurs hadn't got in the way. Isn't that right, Chloe?'

Simon blinks at her a few times. Then he says,

'Why would someone do what you do, Nadine? It's so odd. What turned you into someone who warns people about other people when you know there's no real danger? I can think of only one reason why a person would do that.'

'Shut up!' Nadine sounds scared suddenly.

'It happened to you, didn't it? That's what's behind this. You were warned away from somebody. At work? In your personal life? You listened, and . . . and then, later, you wished you hadn't. The person who gave you the advice might have done so because they cared – maybe too much – but they were wrong. You suffered as a result. You lost something – something you cared deeply about. It must have felt like losing everything.'

'Interesting story,' Nadine says in a brittle voice. She looks away, towards the door to the balcony. 'See, Chloe? He feels free to make up stories about me while accusing me of making stuff up about Tom Rigbey.'

I clear my throat. 'Nadine, if Simon's got you all wrong, tell me what it is about Tom that makes you think he's a plague and not to be trusted. It's your opinion – fine – but what are you basing it on?'

'I was just trying to warn you, Chloe,' she snaps. 'For your own sake. I wish I hadn't bothered.'

'But why did you feel the need to warn me?' For some reason, in spite of everything, I want to give her one last chance. I don't want to condemn anybody on weak evidence. Not Tom, certainly, but no one else either.

'How can I talk to you now, Chloe?' Nadine demands, as if I've let her down badly. 'You're engaged to *him*. You've made it very clear whose side you're on. Anything I say now will fall on deaf ears.'

Simon stands up. 'Let's go, Chloe. She won't tell you anything because there's nothing to tell.'

'Chloe's not so sure about that, DC Simon. Are you, Chloe?'

'Yes,' I say. 'Yes, I am. Get some help, Nadine. I'm sorry if you've had a bad experience, but it's not my fault, or Tom's. Stop trying to ruin other people's happiness.'

'That's right,' says Nadine bitterly as Simon and I turn to leave. 'You tell yourself *I'm* the one doing that. You believe exactly what suits you, like everyone always does.'

17

'Where do you want me to drop you?' Simon asks. We're in his car, driving away from Nadine's house. *Thank God.*

'I don't,' I say. 'Just . . . drive around for a bit. I need to ask you some questions.'

'Ask away.'

'You honestly believe Nadine Caspian is . . . what? A serial warner – like some people are serial killers? She warns one person after another, just for the sake of it? And that's *all* she does? She warns people about other people? Is that a thing? Have you ever known anyone else do that?'

Simon sighs. 'Yes. That's what she is. And no, it's a new one for me. But I've known lots of sick, unhappy people who have taken something that wasn't a thing and never should have become one, and turned it into their own personal way of harming people.'

'All those questions you asked me about Tom – had he told me he'd been fired . . .'

'I wanted you to focus on what you knew for sure. You had no reason to think Tom had been fired. You knew that Nadine had – that other receptionist had told you. I was hoping you'd see that, in the absence of any other facts, that one alone ought to make you more suspicious of Nadine than of Tom.'

'And . . . when you said it was good that I'd had dinner with Tom and accepted his marriage proposal, when you told me to reply to his text as if nothing was wrong . . .'

'I didn't want him to find out that you had doubts about him, planted in your head by Nadine. Most people don't take kindly to being suspected of every sin under the sun when they've done nothing to deserve it. If you'd started acting cold and aloof with Tom, it might have ruined a promising new relationship.'

'I wish you'd told me as soon as you knew,' I say as we drive past the Vue cinema on East Road. 'Why didn't you?'

'I have a way of doing things.'

I wonder if anyone has ever been warned about DC Simon Waterhouse.

'Nadine's right about one thing,' he says. 'It's something people often do when they care about others, or imagine they care. They warn them. Maybe they shouldn't.'

'Maybe not. Unless a heavy boulder is about to land on someone's head.'

'You can't tell people how they ought to feel about other people,' says Simon. 'It doesn't work. Have you and Lorna been best friends for a long time?'

The mention of Lorna's name surprises me. For once, she wasn't in my thoughts at all.

'Yes. It feels like for ever. Why?'

'No reason. Don't worry, I'm not going to warn you about her.'

'Because you don't think she's bad for me, or because Nadine Caspian's put you off warning anyone about anything ever?' I ask.

'I like your suspicious mind,' he says. 'I warn you: carry on like that and you might end up working for the police. She asked me to drop you off at her house after our visit to Nadine.'

'Who did? Lorna?'

He nods.

'No. Drop me off at my . . .' I change my mind mid-sentence. 'Actually, can you drop me off at CamEgo? I want to see Tom, as soon as possible.'

'No problem.'

As I climb out of the car, my phone buzzes twice in my pocket. A message. I wait until I've waved Simon off, then pull out my phone, praying it's a text from Tom.

It is. Four words – 'A mouthful of fish! T xx' – attached to a photo so gross that I'm amazed he dared send it. His mouth is wide open and there's half of what looks like a tuna sandwich stuffed inside it, hanging out because it won't all fit in.

It's not the salmon fillet from earlier, but I suppose tuna will do as evidence. Eating fish did happen, and here's the picture to prove it: a gross one that would put some women off, perhaps, but not me.

I love Tom Rigbey, and I'm going to marry him. He could push a little old lady under a bus tomorrow, or have the flag of a barren country ruled by a dictator tattooed on his face, and my feelings wouldn't change. He could pretend to be a vampire, an arthritic elephant or William the Conqueror reborn and I would still love him every bit as much as I do now.

About the Author

Sophie Hannah is an internationally bestselling writer of psychological crime fiction, published in more than 30 countries.

In 2013 her novel, *The Carrier*, won the Crime Thriller of the Year Award at the Specsavers National Book Awards. Two of Sophie's crime novels, *The Point of Rescue* and *The Other Half Lives*, have been adapted for television and appeared on ITV1 under the series title *Case Sensitive* in 2011 and 2012.

Her latest books are *The Telling Error*, and a brand new Hercule Poirot novel, *The Monogram Murders*.

Hidden	Barbara Taylor Bradford
How to Change Your Life in 7 Steps	John Bird
Humble Pie	Gordon Ramsay
Jack and Jill	Lucy Cavendish
Kung Fu Trip	Benjamin Zephaniah
Last Night Another Soldier	Andy McNab
Life's New Hurdles	Colin Jackson
Life's Too Short	Val McDermid, Editor
The Little One	Lynda La Plante
Love is Blind	Kathy Lette
Men at Work	Mike Gayle
Money Magic	Alvin Hall
One Good Turn	Chris Ryan
Out of the Dark	Adèle Geras
Paris for One	Jojo Moyes
The Perfect Holiday	Cathy Kelly
The Perfect Murder	Peter James
Pictures Or It Didn't Happen	Sophie Hannah
Quantum of Tweed: The Man with the Nissan Micra	Conn Iggulden
Red for Revenge	Fanny Blake
Rules for Dating a Romantic Hero	Harriet Evans
A Sea Change	Veronica Henry
Star Sullivan	Maeve Binchy
Street Cat Bob	James Bowen
Tackling Life	Charlie Oatway
The 10 Keys to Success	John Bird
Today Everything Changes	Andy McNab
Traitors of the Tower	Alison Weir
Trouble on the Heath	Terry Jones
Twenty Tales from the War Zone	John Simpson
We Won the Lottery	Danny Buckland
Wrong Time, Wrong Place	Simon Kernick

Discover the pleasure of reading with Galaxy®

Curled up on the sofa,
 Sunday morning in pyjamas,
just before bed,
 in the bath or
on the way to work?

Wherever, whenever,
 you can escape
with a good book!

So go on...
 indulge yourself with
a good read and the
 smooth taste of
Galaxy® chocolate.

Proudly
supports

Read more at ⨍ Galaxy Chocolate

Quick Reads are brilliant short new books written by bestselling writers to help people discover the joys of reading for pleasure.

Find out more at **www.quickreads.org.uk**

🐦 @Quick_Reads   f Quick-Reads

We would like to thank all our funders:

LOTTERY FUNDED

We would also like to thank all our partners in the Quick Reads project for their help and support: NIACE, unionlearn, National Book Tokens, The Reading Agency, National Literacy Trust, Welsh Books Council, The Big Plus Scotland, DELNI, NALA

At Quick Reads, World Book Day and World Book Night we want to encourage everyone in the UK and Ireland to read more and discover the joy of books.

World Book Day is on 5 March 2015
Find out more at **www.worldbookday.com**

World Book Night is on 23 April 2015
Find out more at **www.worldbooknight.org**

Quick Reads

Start a new chapter

Out of the Dark

Adèle Geras

Rob Stone comes back from the horrors of the First
World War with a ruined face and a broken heart.
Lonely, unable to forget the things he has seen, and
haunted by the ghost of his dead captain, all that
Rob has left is a picture of the captain's family.
Rob sets out to find them, hoping that by giving
them the picture, he can bring peace to the
captain's ghost – and to his own troubled heart.

Quercus

Quick Reads

Start a new chapter

Red for Revenge

Fanny Blake

Two women, one man: code red for revenge...

Maggie is married with two grown-up children.
Her twenty-five-year-old marriage
to Phil has lost its sparkle.

Carla is widowed. She understands life is short
so she lives it to the full. But is her new romance
all that it seems?

When the two women meet in the beauty salon,
they soon find they have more in common
than the colour of their nails.

The discovery that they are sharing the same
man is shocking. How will Phil be taught
a lesson or two he won't forget?

Orion

Start a new chapter

Dead Man Talking

Roddy Doyle

Pat had been best friends with Joe Murphy
since they were kids. But five years ago
they had a fight. A big one, and they haven't
spoken since – till the day before Joe's funeral.
What? On the day before his funeral
Joe would be dead, wouldn't he?
Yes, he would…

Jonathan Cape

Quick Reads

Start a new chapter

Paris for One

Jojo Moyes

Nell is twenty-six and has never been to Paris.
She has never even been on a weekend away with
her boyfriend. Everyone knows she is just
not the adventurous type.

But, when her boyfriend doesn't turn up
for their romantic mini-break, Nell has the
chance to prove everyone wrong.

Alone in Paris, Nell meets the mysterious moped-
riding Fabien and his group of carefree friends.

Could this turn out to be the most
adventurous weekend of her life?

Michael Joseph

Start a new chapter

Street Cat Bob

James Bowen

When James Bowen found an injured street cat
in the hallway of his sheltered housing, he had no
idea just how much his life was about to change.
James had been living on the streets of London
and the last thing he needed was a pet.

Yet James couldn't resist the clever tom cat,
whom he quickly named Bob. Soon the two were
best friends, and their funny and sometimes dangerous
adventures would change both their lives, slowly
healing the scars of each other's troubled pasts.

Street Cat Bob is a moving and uplifting story
that will touch the heart of anyone who reads it.

Hodder & Stoughton

Why not start a reading group?

If you have enjoyed this book, why not share your next Quick Read with friends, colleagues, or neighbours.

A reading group is a great way to get the most out of a book and is easy to arrange. All you need is a group of people, a place to meet and a date and time that works for everyone.

Use the first meeting to decide which book to read first and how the group will operate. Conversation doesn't have to stick rigidly to the book. Here are some suggested themes for discussions:

- How important was the plot?

- What messages are in the book?

- Discuss the characters – were they believable and could you relate to them?

- How important was the setting to the story?

- Are the themes timeless?

- Personal reactions – what did you like or not like about the book?

There is a free toolkit with lots of ideas to help you run a Quick Reads reading group at **www.quickreads.org.uk**

Share your experiences of your group on Twitter 🐦 @Quick_Reads

For more ideas, offers and groups to join visit Reading Groups for Everyone at **www.readingagency.org.uk/readinggroups**

Other resources

Enjoy this book?

Find out about all the others at **www.quickreads.org.uk**

For Quick Reads audio clips as well as videos
and ideas to help you enjoy reading visit the
BBC's Skillswise website **www.bbc.co.uk/quickreads**

Join the Reading Agency's Six Book Challenge at
www.readingagency.org.uk/sixbookchallenge

THE
READING
AGENCY

Find more books for new readers at
www.newisland.ie
www.barringtonstoke.co.uk

Free courses to develop your skills are available in your
local area. To find out more phone 0800 100 900.

For more information on developing your skills
in Scotland visit **www.thebigplus.com**

Want to read more? Join your local library. You can borrow
books for free and take part in inspiring reading activities.